*American
Wives*

The

Iowa

Short

Fiction

Award

University of

Iowa Press

Iowa City

*Beth
Helms*

*American
Wives*

University of Iowa Press, Iowa City 52242

Printed in the United States of America

http://www.uiowa.edu/uiowapress

The publication of this book was generously supported by the
University of Iowa Foundation and the National Endowment
for the Arts.

Printed on acid-free paper

Library of Congress Cataloging-in-Publication Data

Helms, Beth, 1965–

American wives / by Beth Helms.

p. cm.—(The Iowa short fiction award)

Contents: American wives — The confines of civilized behavior —
Men in Italy — Oysters — Collected stories — Once — Telling
stories — Glazing — Antique map collecting.

ISBN 0-87745-868-5 (pbk.)

1. Americans — Foreign countries — Fiction. I. Title. II. Series.

PS3608.E465A83 2003

813'. 6 — dc21   2003042644

03 04 05 06 07 P 5 4 3 2 1

For my parents,

who watch from somewhere with astonishment

Contents

ACKNOWLEDGMENTS

My thanks to Vermont College and especially to
   François Camoin and Nance Van Winckel.
Endless gratitude to the writers who first
   encouraged me, Kate Walbert and Peter Rock.
Most of all, my thanks to Gary for his support
   and patience.
And love to my three beautiful almost-
   daughters: Lauren, Lindsay, and Jessie-cat.

*American
Wives*

American Wives

In Germany, following the little war in the Middle East, life settles down. Mary Frances adjusts: to her husband's schedule and the sunless apartment, to the landscape of a new foreign city. Baghdad had a strange, concrete architecture; flat, squatting facades dotted with wild touches — an orange balcony, an avocado railing. Frankfurt is a grim, industrial city but still offers sudden surprises — a cobbled street, a gingerbread trim. Two months ago, Mary Frances and Charles were evacuated with the other Americans and reassigned to Frankfurt. They had been allowed just three suitcases. There is still some question about their household goods, whether they will ever see them again.

In Baghdad there had been palm trees and an orange and lemon tree in the walled garden, faded rugs against cool tiled floors. Now their apartment is on a busy thoroughfare; the tram rattles by right outside the kitchen window. The streets are filled with sturdily built people clomping about on errands, bundled in coats and mufflers, hats and gloves. The snow falls like any other snow but becomes filthy in a matter of moments. Mary Frances comes in from her day's business with salty, slushy shoes and a feeling of grime on her face and in her hair.

She is surprised to find herself missing Baghdad, its heady foreign smells — of lamb roasting, of dried apricots, sticky dates — and lush vegetation, the beauty of its women suggested, even enhanced, by the veils that swayed beneath their eyes, as if they were too lovely for the eyes of men. Here no one looks at her when she walks down the street. In Baghdad she wore a scarf as a gesture of respect; now she wears it only for fashion and to protect her hair.

In the Middle East, she had not minded the dress code — wives had been urged to be respectful — and she would not have thought to wear slacks into the street. One morning though — they had been in Baghdad less than a month then — Jess had fallen over in her high chair, and Mary Frances, by some chance dressed all in white — white slacks and sleeveless top, white patent sandals — had run the entire way to the embassy, holding the bleeding, screaming child. By the time she arrived they were both covered with blood, in a dozen different shades. In the busy morning streets, men had stepped slowly aside but with exaggerated insolence, as though making room was a capitulation, an undeserved favor. Some called out things that sounded threatening, even obscene. She had rattled at the gates of the embassy; a group of men and women had gathered to watch and they stood too close, crowding her, until the Marine — erect, white-gloved, stoic — stepped from the guard booth. He opened the gates with infuriating caution, his eyes guarded.

She had made quite a scene, Charles told her later, disapprovingly. Quite a scene. The injury to Jess, of course, had been mostly blood and hysteria. Two tiny stitches were sewn into her lower lip by a young GI doctor.

Now a woman named Ingrid cleans the apartment twice a week. She helps with Jess, who is no longer in a high chair and will go to nursery school in the fall. Ingrid brooks no pickiness or disobedience from children. When Jess refuses to eat, Ingrid simply leans the chair back and stuffs her like a Strasbourg goose. Jess is too shocked to argue or cry; she must use all her energy to breathe through her nose.

In the spring, Mary Frances signs up for night school at the university: "Beginning German," taught by a serious young man in tweed jackets, smoking one cigarette after another. Klaus is the instructor's name, and he stalks the head of the room in a distracted way while the class watches him, still dressed in their outdoor clothes. Though the heating pipes rattle and clang, they provide no perceptible warmth. None comes from Klaus either, whose teaching manner is disdainful, and who immediately sought out two pallid British girls and made them his favorites. In the evenings, twice each week, Mary Frances wedges her knees beneath a scarred desk and tries to follow Klaus's clipped lessons. The classes are held in a bright bare room; the university feels like an institute. Mary Frances thinks of the word *polytechnic*. Nothing here is pretty on purpose; anything attractive seems accidental, incidental, slightly subversive. A flowering tree bursting up through the sidewalk, sprinkling pale blossoms, or the way the evening light ripples the fountain near the zoo — these seem so out of place that she half-waits for someone to notice them and take them away, to uproot the tree, drain the fountain.

German makes her brain hurt. Charles speaks it fluently. His gift for languages is eerie; his ear is keen and perfect. Nights when he's not too tired, he corrects her pronunciation, unravels for her the tangles of irregular verbs, the bewildering exceptions. He seems to understand that his talent for the minutiae, the complexity of language, is not normal, or even quite human.

Why are you doing this, he asked one night. Why bother?

Because, Mary Frances wanted to tell him, I won't be another army wife, with my brain going to soup, shopping for clocks and Hanover china. Sipping coffee, nibbling kuchen in yet another living room. That night, though, she had just stared at him and shrugged.

She seeks out German friends, German restaurants, and when the time comes, she enrolls Jess in a German nursery school, shocking the other wives, whose children all attend the American program. Among these women there is a carefully observed hierarchy, a tentative camaraderie where closeness is dependent on — dictated by — the ranks of their assorted husbands. Like the men, the women flock together in strict accordance with the military's prescribed rankings: the wives of the warrant officers socialize together; the chief warrant officers' wives form an entirely different clique. For all that, though, they are much the same — gossipy as magpies, bone weary from the effort of keeping up appearances. Now that the thrill of a new city has worn thin, they pour coffee and complain — about the cosmetics they can't find, the prices, the help.

In the evenings there are endless social functions to attend. There is a joyless quality to these gatherings, a false sparkle in the conversation, the urgent consumption of alcohol.

Standing at one such party, Mary Frances listens to the women comparing tours of duty: Germany versus where they were last, where they think they might go next. All the past countries, even the hardship posts, seem to have taken on a retroactive prettiness; they speak of these places with dreamy nostalgia, as if recalling beautiful childhoods.

Mary Frances does it too, speaking of Baghdad as if it were an exotic garden rather than a city in which she had spent a mere four months. As though there had not been the incident with the high chair, or the war and the evacuation in the middle of the night — across the desert to Tehran in open trucks, the canvas flapping eerily overhead, the women hushed and frightened, huddled together, frantic about their husbands, their left belongings. All the children had been terribly sick, ill with some local intestinal ailment they couldn't fight; several infants had died. When Mary Frances remembers these things, she regrets the conversations she's just had over drinks in someone's living room — the telling, lovely and false.

———————

Klaus, the German teacher, is thin and pale. When Mary Frances catches up with him outside class one evening, she notices that he blinks frequently, as though the outside world is unfamiliar, possibly dangerous. He walks quickly, a thick book un der each arm. Mary Frances touches the book he carries, pressing it down a little with her hand; it seems to her more appropriate than touching his sleeve. Up close, walking beside him, she notices the wispy hairs he's missed shaving, a nick under his chin, a smell of stale beer. His clothes look rumpled, even slept-in. She imagines that underneath them he is pale and thin from head to toe, nearly hairless, with the body of a boy. He must be close to her own age, but he carries himself with an air of authority she attributes to his proficiency in her language as well as his own. This knowledge feels like a secret she needs to get out of him, for her own purposes.

When she asks about private tutoring, he says nothing for so long a time that she wonders if he heard her. They are walking in the city proper now; the university is surrounded by it, and one can step in and out almost without noticing. Steam billows from the grates. They pass a bakery, restaurants, street vendors. Scents drift from the doorways: sauerkraut and beer, the thick smell of bread; she hears music — a lively, silly sort of polka — from an open window above them. The streetlights curve overhead in graceful arms; they make the street appear shiny, moon-tinted.

She points out a man selling seashells filled with a thick, sweet substance the consistency of honey. "Jess — my little girl — loves those," she tells him.

Klaus glances at her. "They are filthy," he says. "I wouldn't advise it."

"I'd like to surprise my husband," Mary Frances says then. "I feel a little at sea with the German. I'm terrible with languages, and he's very good."

"Your husband is with the American army?"

"That's right. He's a language whiz, a *wunderkind*." She says this confidingly, feeling suddenly that she is convincing him of something, or that she must try. The word *wunderkind*, she realizes quickly, was a mistake — the slangy use of his own language, in his own country. This makes her feel tacky, common, American.

But he does not seem to notice or take offense. "Did you live in California?" he says.

"As a matter of fact, yes. How did you know?"

Klaus shrugs his slight shoulders; the ill-fitting jacket doesn't settle back properly but rides above and away from his neck, exaggerating the impression that he is a boy dressed in a man's clothing.

"You saw the ocean every day then? What is that like?"

Mary Frances matches her pace to his; they are striding down the uneven pavement like a couple with a schedule, appointments to keep.

"Pretty," she says. "Dull after a while, believe it or not."

Klaus does not seem to; he shoots her a glance that is strangely contemptuous, even hostile. "I am quite busy," he says. "I attend classes as well as teaching them."

"Where are you studying?"

"I am studying a number of things."

Mary Frances feels slapped. She says nothing but thinks: what a rude, unattractive, fishy-eyed boy you are. I'm sorry I asked; sorry I bothered.

Then, unexpectedly, he says, "I could meet you in the afternoons, twice a week. What is your address?"

He stops suddenly and faces her. The crowds part around them, pass and join again, fluidly.

"Should you write it down?" Mary Frances fumbles with her handbag, intending to search for a pen, a scrap of paper.

"No need," he says and then blinks rapidly as she recites the address. He seems to be processing the information in a peculiar, robotic way.

Walking home, she wonders how wise an idea this was; it had come over her suddenly during class, while her mind was reeling with German articles. Nothing she is learning is staying put; she feels fuzzy brained and stupid. Even the British girls are cleverer, better at remembering strange rules, rolling their mouths around the new guttural words. At night Charles is no longer so inclined to help her; he is increasingly frustrated with her inability to understand simple things. He complains too of the job here; the evacuation from Baghdad has sidetracked him, set him back. He had been hoping for a more exotic post — Morocco perhaps, or Saudi Arabia. But his complaints are vague and unspecific, and if she questions him further, he looks at her blankly, as if the idea of explaining it all is too exhausting to contemplate.

He prefers to bathe Jess, to sit on the floor of her room and play with the toy airplane he brought her from a recent trip, with its flashing red lights and satisfying engine noises. Recently, he has been traveling more and more. The calls come in the middle of the night, and he rises and picks up his bag, kept packed in the hall closet, and walks out into the night, bound for anywhere. He cannot or will not tell her where he is going; this is another subject of conversation among the wives, those whose husbands disappear in the night. When might they return? If two or more wives are missing husbands at the same time, they will enjoy a brief closeness, forming a small group at coffees or in church, saying to each other in low voices: Have you heard anything? Have you had a call?

"Give up the German, why don't you," Charles had suggested before he left. He was sitting on the carpet, surrounded by Jess's animals, both wooden and stuffed. Jess takes the clothes off the dolls and dresses the animals in them — bears in frilly skirts, a duck in lederhosen.

"It's a very difficult language," he said. "As difficult as English."

"I've had no problem with English. I'm almost fluent." But it was a weak joke and she was on the verge of tears.

"Now, now," he had said. And then to Jess, pointing at the animals one by one, "*Ein bär. Ein ente. Ein pferd.*"

At a restaurant one night with another American couple, Jess slides off her chair and disappears under the tablecloth. For a time Mary Frances is aware of the small body near her feet, the feel of a smocked little chest against her stockinged ankle. This is why, she thinks, children should stay home with babysitters until they are old enough to use cutlery, fold their napkins, sit upright.

There is a scream then, from several tables away, a mingling of noise in which she can make out Jess's indignant, frightened cry, as well as the voice of a woman and the high-pitched barking of a dog. There is confusion; chairs are scraped back; waiters crowd in and retreat.

When Jess has been found several tables away and retrieved, and rapid German spoken fluently by Charles and the woman, while Mary Frances stands nearby studying Jess's small hand, the puncture wounds on the soft heel, it becomes clear what has happened. The woman brings a small dachshund onto her lap and speaks in an angry flurry of German. Mary Frances, incensed but speechless, stands helplessly nearby, dabbing the bite with a linen napkin. Jess whimpers but doesn't cry — she seems more shocked than injured.

"Shots," she hears herself say over and over again to Charles. "Has it had its shots?"

There is another exchange in German. Charles turns to her and smiles broadly. He says to her, "Fraulein wants to know if the little girl has had hers."

"That's not funny," says Mary Frances in English, and then tries again in German. It doesn't come out and the woman stares at her blankly before returning to her table, hoisting the dog in her lap and speaking again to her companions in quick, angry tones.

The evening is ruined. Jess is inconsolable. She'd been trying to make friends, she says over and over again. Trying to make friends. It isn't until later that Mary Frances will realize Jess had spoken these words in German, with complete ease, her babyish tones sliding over the harsh sounds, making them sweet.

When she sees him next, she tells this to Klaus, with the thought of entertaining him. Twice a week he arrives, sits at the flimsy table in the kitchen and snaps open books. His rap at the door is businesslike and efficient. Jess is in the Wonderland nursery school now until early afternoon, when Ingrid will pick her up and walk her home. They have one uninterrupted hour, a little more. Klaus will not accept anything she offers him. Coffee, pastries, Coca-Colas, stories.

What did she want from him after all? Not this. He is brisk and demanding of her, moderating himself only when he notices that she is pained or embarrassed. Then he blushes, ducks his head and mutters not an apology but a defense, a weary accusation. "We have done this," he will say. "Last week and the one before also."

Mary Frances feels, accurately, that she has not lessened but doubled the disappointment she is causing others. Charles, thankfully, no longer asks about her German lessons. He is under pressure, he says, bucking for a promotion, another appointment.

Months go by, and summer — too quick, too pale — passes.

She and Charles take Jess on weekend trips to Cologne, to Strasbourg and Vienna. Photographic evidence mounts; Mary Frances fills the paper pages of photo albums with endless cathedrals and overflowing window boxes — elusive gingerbread memories. No wonder, then, that the recollections of the wives will later be so pleasant, so gold-tinged — this is what they choose to record. These are the images they select and paste carefully down, thumbing the edges with precision, writing captions underneath: *Mary Frances, Charles, Jess. Hamburg, Germany, March 1970. Cold!*

Her German lessons continue, though no great progress is made. She and Klaus reach a grim, unspoken pact — neither will quit, despite her obvious lack of aptitude, his growing annoyance. Her pronunciation, he tells her, is quite awful. When Mary Frances tries out a new phrase on Ingrid, Ingrid merely sniffs and adds more muscle to her dusting or stirring or sweeping. Her broad back hides her contempt, or her amusement. With Charles, Mary Frances has stopped speaking German entirely.

In the fall Charles is sent to the States on temporary duty; he will be gone at least a month. The days are long, tedious. Watery sunlight streams through the windows; standing in the living room she can see it catch the colored glass stones that stud the wall around the courtyard. Jess spends hours there, prying them loose, burying them in various places. Mary Frances assumes she believes them valuable, and they are deceptively pretty — colors like ruby, aquamarine, topaz. In Charles's absence, Mary Frances successfully teaches Jess to play Go Fish. Ingrid, stoic, silent, vaguely belligerent, cleans the house with soldierly efficiency, cooks mysterious stews and roulades, and leaves Mary Frances the warming directions written in stilted English.

Accidents happen. Jess gets her foot stuck in the elevator door and watches her knee travel toward her face with accelerating speed. There is hysteria while Mary Frances pounds on the steel doors, and then Jess, just five, has the presence of mind to press the emergency button. Jess's German grows on par with her English; now she leads her mother into bakeries and orders bread and pastries, delighting the shopkeepers. On the fringe of these conversations, Mary Frances smiles and nods. Her child is charming; her German is delightful. This much she understands.

On the advice of another wife, she begins taking pills prescribed by an American doctor at the hospital. She described to him a vague anxiety, a restless boredom that makes her want to jump out of her skin. The uniformed doctor — so young, so uninterested — had scribbled something on a scrap of paper and handed it to her, not even meeting her eyes. How many of us must he see, she wondered. How many of us, bored brittle, walking around with such great care, afraid we might shatter, literally shatter?

There is no word from Charles, but this is not surprising. When the phone rings it's another military wife, wanting to scare up a card game, a coffee, a shopping trip.

While Charles is gone, Mary Frances begins letting Jess go to the bakery alone. She is too tired to dress, and the effort it takes seems overwhelming. It doesn't occur to her that a five-year-old walking half a block alone is suspect in any way, or in danger. No, she is only annoyed to walk out onto the front step and find Jess there, hollowing out the loaf of bread, stuffing the soft parts into her mouth, watching people go by. She retrieves the crust, lifts Jess to her feet by the hood of her coat, and takes her inside.

In the afternoons she drowses under the window in the living room, pleasantly stoned from the pills. Jess plays at her feet, a made-up, one-handed game of Go Fish, or the kind of solitaire where the cards are arranged like a clock. Sometimes she wakes to find Jess gone entirely and will look out the window, with a moment's anxiety, to find her playing in the courtyard, arranging her glass treasures.

Klaus comes one day when she'd forgotten he was due. She is still in her bathrobe and nightgown, her hair in disarray, eyes sticky. Ingrid has the week off, and ashtrays litter the apartment; unwashed dishes are piled on the kitchen table. When he steps inside his disapproval is obvious; it pierces the fuzzy well-being that the pills have been so competently providing. Klaus — his ill-fitting clothes and German rectitude — brings her to her senses; with mounting embarrassment, she looks around the room and then down at her dressing gown.

"Hold on," she says and hurries into the bedroom. She rinses her face and runs a comb through her hair. She comes back and collects ashtrays on her way to the kitchen, where Klaus is now standing, eyes on some point above the mess, still holding his books.

"Sorry, sorry," she says. "I forgot, I'm afraid. Completely slipped my mind."

"Not to worry," he says, with unnatural gallantry. As if to reinforce this he puts his books down on an empty chair and moves a dirty dish from the table to the sink.

"Sit please," she says. "I'll make coffee."

"Where is the little girl?" asks Klaus.

"Jesus," says Mary Frances, thinking. She reties her dressing gown, buys a little time. "At the zoo, of course," she says with relief, as this fact resolves itself in her mind. If Klaus is here it is Tuesday, and she remembers signing a permission slip. "There was a field trip to the zoo. With her class."

Klaus, too, seems relieved. He sits down at the table and beats a little rhythm on the underside.

"Charles is in the States," she tells him, cleaning around his chair. She sweeps crumbs into a dish towel, scrubs at a stain near his shoe.

"Ah," says Klaus and nods. It is not clear what he understands. Perhaps he is just willing to accept a man's absence as a reasonable excuse for slovenliness.

Mary Frances lifts the filmed dishes from the table and hides them in the sink. The room smells of neglect — old food, souring milk, an odor that has been there all week, but it is Klaus's presence that brings it to her attention. She lifts the window, forgetting for a moment that Frankfurt air smells of grime.

Finally he says, "Will you sit please?" He has been flipping the pages of his book, tapping his fingers, and patting the sides of the coffee cup she put in front of him. The steam has subsided, but he has not lifted it from the table. Mary Frances drops the dish towel and sinks into the chair beside him.

"Oh for goodness' sake," she says with a little laugh. "I think I might cry."

"You do not look well," he says. "I think you are missing your husband."

"It's this city," she says. "Forgive me. It's depressing me terribly. I'm low all the time. I can't concentrate for beans."

Klaus seems puzzled, but this look is directed at the tabletop, not at her. Finally he says, "Well. After you see the ocean so much, maybe this is understandable."

She laughs. "I don't think that's it at all. You don't find this city gray? Sorrowful? Bleak?"

"Frankfurt?" he says. "No, I do not."

She is aware she has insulted him. She waves a hand. "Never mind," she says. "I'm talking nonsense. Where did we leave off?"

But Klaus has shut his books now and is looking at her seriously. "I cannot continue to teach you," he says. "This, in fact, is what I have come to say today. Perhaps you did not realize that it isn't our day for studying? Today is Friday."

Mary Frances shakes her head a little. She runs a hand across her eyes. "I beg your pardon? What are you saying?"

Now Klaus studies a collection of children's dishes on the counter. A Peter Rabbit mug and bowl — the only way she can get Jess to eat when Ingrid isn't around is by tricking her into digging down to the pattern. Find the bunnies, she'll beg, coaxing Jess along, a spoonful at a time. At the bottom of the dish, the bunnies — as impeccably dressed as Jess's own animals — are having a perpetual bonfire in Mr. McGregor's garden.

Klaus says, "It is not appropriate, I've realized, for this to be taking place."

"What? What is taking place?" She puts her hand on his sleeve — corduroy worn almost transparent. "I don't mean to be stupid, but I don't understand."

He looks at her hand and puts his own on top of it. His hand is spidery and pale; dark hairs sprout from the knuckles. "This is what I mean," he says thickly. His eyes are glittering; a flush is climbing his face.

"Oh Klaus," she says, removing her hand quickly. "You don't understand. I wasn't intending anything. You've misunderstood. Please don't think I had thoughts of you, of that kind."

"It is not your thoughts I am speaking of," he says. She feels his hand on the slick material of her dressing gown, near her knee. His touch is not gentle; he holds her knee grimly and squeezes. His fingers knead back and forth. She feels a sickening sort of excitement; something turns in her stomach. His face is very close. Beery breath, flared nostrils. He seems feral to her now, a little dangerous.

She pulls in a ragged breath, sits up straighter and leans away. His hand has traveled up her leg, found skin under the slippery blue fabric. He fastens his hard mouth onto her neck and moans. He is everywhere suddenly — hot, moist, clutching. She feels revulsion, heat, helplessness. She pushes the chair back and stands up; his grip is still firm on her thigh and he is saying things to her: silly, cruel, adolescent things. She thinks, how does he know all these words, these ugly phrases, in English? She takes his hand and pries it from her leg.

She says, "Stop it. Stop it at once." The coffee has gone over, making a trickling brown waterfall onto the linoleum. She goes to the sink to fetch a towel.

He slumps against his chair, puffing a little. She watches him, holding the sopping towel in her hand.

She touches his hair, "Poor Klaus," she says. "Poor Klaus. Come on, let's think of something else."

He puts his arms around her waist, burrows his head against her chest and holds her fiercely.

"There," she says foolishly. "There, there."

"I am not a child," he says angrily. "I am not a teenager."

It's true, of course. This is how she has thought of him. His fragile wrists and ankles; his doughy skin and inadequate shaves. Even his stiff formality had seemed to her youthful and put on.

"Oh all right," she says after a moment. She lets herself be pulled onto his lap. "Take it easy, though. Go easy."

He can't seem to help himself; he is all jabbing fingers and sharpness. Angles and bones. Still, Mary Frances feels more clearheaded than she has in days. She feels charitable and generous, dispensing kindness, giving something that costs nothing. She widens her bare legs, winds her arms around his thin neck.

Afterward, adjusting herself — the nightgown has become twisted into hot, sweaty coils around her waist — she glances at the clock. It is nearly four in the afternoon. Something nags at her. Klaus is composed now; that boy, that desperate hard-fingered boy, is gone. He strokes his books absently, stares out the window. He does not seem inclined to move.

Jess. Mary Frances looks up, around. "What day did you say it was?" she asks slowly.

"It's Friday."

"Friday. The trip to the zoo is Tuesday. Next Tuesday."

Running down the street that afternoon, dressed in what she could find, could lay her hands on quickly, she threaded and pushed through a maze of solid shoulders and backs. Her shoes rang on the metal grates; the uneven pavement tripped her up, sent her stumbling. All the way there she was not thinking of Jess, not really; instead she was thinking of the way Klaus had stared at her across the sticky table — in a way that stole away all the easy, magnanimous feelings she had earned just short moments before.

She was thinking of what he had said.

You American wives. You are all the same.

There had been the smell of cold, spilled coffee and gravy from two nights before; the radio was playing Wagner. There was a strangely clean breeze from the open window. It ruffled the curtains and caressed the hairs on the back of her neck. When she looked at him he was examining her coldly, while lighting a cigarette.

———————

Four years passed in Germany. Leaving Frankfurt, Mary Frances found that among the things they had collected — buffets and dining furniture, marble-topped commodes, delicate Christmas ornaments and chiming clocks — she had also acquired fairly competent conversational German. How much of this can be attributed to Klaus she does not know.

She does remember that she had dressed Jess up for Charles's return. Ingrid had cleaned and cooked, and Mary Frances had hidden her pills. She hadn't dared take one since that horrible afternoon with Klaus. Jess was fine, of course, miserable and frightened and waiting at the nursery school to be picked up, but fine in all the important ways.

Oh baby, Mary Frances said to her, oh honey. Mommy's so sorry.

When Charles came through the door, he smelled of that peculiar Frankfurt cold. It was caught in the folds of his coat and under his collar; it filled the hollows of his ears and throat. She put her face in those places for a good long time.

These days, Mary Frances recalls that autumn afternoon more charitably. Like her photo albums, which show only castles and churches and window boxes tumbling with flowers, Mary Frances sees her younger self as gracious, and Klaus as grateful, sweet and awed.

Everything else is erased — that he found her shallow, a poor student and a worse mother. She doesn't remember his censuring eyes, the soiled table, her stained polyester nightgown. For if she allowed these things, even so many years later, she would know that what happened between them could not have been possible.

The
Confines of
Civilized
Behavior

All afternoon the girls play tirelessly in the pool. The nanny half-reclines on a teak bench near its shallow end. In the sunlight her belly-button ring — the figure of a man climbing her torso — winks. The tiny man holds a jewel in his teeth; his arms stretch upward, as if seeking a handhold. The nanny is only twenty and she is very, very tall — taller than most men. Her eyes are mostly closed, but still I trust her with the children.

Lying there like that, with her neck propped up unnaturally, arms at her sides, shirt riding below her breasts, she might not even be breathing. A wasp buzzes her, skimming the bits of hair that rise up from her face in the heat; then it lands tentatively on her wrist bone. She doesn't move. Over the past two or three hours, as I've passed her — handing out drinks or wiping faces with towels — the skin on her arms has browned noticeably. I will tease her soon, about how she's ready to be served. Crisp. I do not believe she's actually asleep. If there were an emergency she would be in the pool in a flash, kicking off her fancy running shoes, wading right into the deep end in her long denim skirt. She has a quiet heroic quality, this lofty German girl who lives with us now.

The men surround the grill, fussing with platters of food, with oversized utensils. The dog is underfoot, almost hysterical. In the kitchen there are cold salads and things waiting to be taken from the refrigerator. Beers are frosted; wine bottles are cold to the touch. My father-in-law — dressed in a windbreaker and dark slacks, black socks and dress shoes — stalks up and down the edge of the lawn with his hands clasped behind him. If he is hot — and he should be on the verge of sunstroke — there is no sign of it.

Earlier the children abandoned a croquet game; the balls are scattered in the green like oversized Easter eggs. There has been so much rain lately that the grass is nearly above the wickets — no doubt this is why the game was forgotten. If I keep moving I can keep from being drawn too deeply into any conversation. I've perfected a way of moving purposefully, always with something in hand, eyes fixed somewhere, wearing a polite half-smile.

On the porch, furniture is arranged for conversation, clusters of white wicker with blue cushions. Blue was chosen to complement the hydrangea, which are so abundant, so freakishly large and healthy, that I cannot cut enough of them. They spill over from the delft-blue vases and bowls; they last for weeks and seem unwilling to die. I hand out clippers before guests depart, urging them to cut armloads to take home.

Now my husband's sister is asking her son not to crawl around on the ground and bark at the dog. I pass her and smile, and though I have been thinking that it is only matter of time before this child is bitten in the face, I have waited for Susan to come to this conclusion on her own. She follows me into the house; from the kitchen I can still hear Alec's high-pitched barking.

"You've lost weight," I tell her. I've said this already, more than once.

"I've been bike riding?" she says and shrugs, as though this weight loss is mysterious to her, as if she hadn't noticed. Now she moves around the kitchen, nervously. It's like being lighter has untethered her somehow, set her adrift. "What can I do to help?"

"I don't know. Look for paper napkins?"

Susan is so diminished that her hair seems enormous around her head, kinked in tight reddish curls. Her breasts are tiny, childish peaks at the front of her T-shirt. Only her backside hasn't really changed. When Simon is feeling cruel and clever he says that one or the other of our girls is getting Susan's ass.

"How's Francie working out?" Susan asks now. Francie is the nanny, the lengthy, supine lovely by my swimming pool.

"Beautifully." I take a bowl of salad from the fridge, set it on the island. "I'm hardly needed anymore." I bare my teeth to show that I'm joking, that I'm not really feeling superseded.

The truth is, I love having Francie here. Francie allows the girls to scramble up and down her body as if she were a telephone pole or a human swing set; Francie makes up games of flashlight tag played in the dark on summer nights. Francie has taught them all the swear words in German, and now I can ignore the cursing in good conscience. Even today, with almost nine months left on her visa, I am thinking up ways of getting around the system.

"Where did she come from again?"

I decide to ignore what I hear in Susan's voice. I say, "Simon met her at a lecture, remember? She's from some tiny place in East Germany."

"That's right. How neat."

"If I'm not worried about it," I say, "I'm not sure why you would be. Can you hand me that? No, the salt."

I remind myself that I'll joke with Simon about this later. Your family thinks you're bonking the au pair, I'll say. We'll giggle about that in the dark, until Simon can't sleep and goes downstairs to read. I'm sure Simon is not sleeping with the nanny; for one thing, the nanny can do better.

At the moment I think Simon is sleeping with my best friend. I believe his relationship with the nanny is one that exists only in his mind — that it is rooted in boyish optimism and ideas of proximity and opportunity.

Now he calls from the porch, and when I do not answer immediately, he comes to find me. Susan does not look at him directly. On the whole, Simon's family veers between opposed sentiments. They fiercely disapprove of him — his apathy toward religion, rumors of his habits and tastes — but they cannot stay away from his swimming pool, the lawns and gardens, the big house, my pastry. We see much more of them in the summer months. It's the classic struggle, Simon says, morality and avarice. Good and venal.

In the kitchen, Simon kisses me theatrically. The kitchen island — an old workbench on wheels — is dislodged and bumps Susan from behind.

"Christ," she says and leaves the kitchen in a hurry.

Simon lifts up an edge of plastic wrap and picks at the salad. He says, "The dog is going to bite my nephew. It's a mathematical certainty."

"Good," I say and put the bowl in his arms. "Out please. Can you ask Francie to come in for a minute? I need to know what to do with this cake of hers."

"My pleasure," he says and rushes away. On the counter is the plum cake Francie has made; it's very beautiful. The plums are perfect half-moons, overlapping. The slicing took her hours.

I hear her behind me; smell the heat of her. I put my arm around her waist and she bends her head so it rests on my hair. "This is so lovely. So much work. You shouldn't have."

I feel her shoulders lift and drop. She makes a noncommittal noise. She is a quiet girl, but it's mostly the language barrier. She's told me she was very lax in studying her English vocabulary; her understanding is acute, her ability to express herself slightly limited.

"It needs sugar," she says and untangles herself to find some.

She bends over the cake, the sifter in her big brown hand, and shakes crystals over the sunset colors of the plums. As we watch, the sugar melts over the sweet of the fruit, leaving just a crystalline shimmer, a pebbly shine.

"Perfect," I tell her, and she smiles down at her work.

―――――――

Later, when we've eaten, when Susan's son has wiped his buttery hands in Francie's silky hair and she has let him, with barely a grimace, we move together to clear the table. Francie works efficiently and steadily, and though this is not her job and I've told her again and again, she cannot seem to help herself. Francie is the kind of girl grown women like to call well brought up.

"Is it me," I ask her in a jokey way, "or is that nephew of mine obnoxious?"

She holds out a strand of her fine hair and lets it fall. "No," she says. "It is not you."

We clean the kitchen and drink wine from big goblets. Francie smokes one of my cigarettes, but furtively, because she doesn't want the children to know about this habit. We heard them go trooping upstairs a little while before; they were headed for my bathtub, where they will pile in and tease and splash each other. When Francie disappeared after them, I knew she was going to spread towels on the floor, around the claw feet of the tub, to prevent another disaster. They are fish, my girls; they can spend the entire day swimming and the rest of the night in the tub, chin deep in bubbles. The tips of their fingers are perpetually deformed and wrinkled; their skin is always damp to the touch. At night they want mermaid hair, and I've taught Francie to do it. She spreads curls across their pillows so they seem like sea-maidens, trailing scarves of kelp.

When the dishes are finished, Francie and I sit quietly at the counter and sip from our glasses. Through the window I hear the beginning of a low whine from Alec that means he's overtired, which will soon signal the end of the evening. Francie and I look at each other and smile a little. She has already left wrapped things on the counter, neat squares of aluminum foil holding slices of cheesecake and blueberry pie. Simon's family, always greedy, never leaves empty-handed.

When they're gone, carrying food and bunches of hydrangea, Simon joins us in the kitchen. He is smoking a cigar, drinking something from a heavy, opaque tumbler.

"Thank God that's over," he says. He holds the cigar out to me, to Francie. We shake our heads. "Girls?" he asks.

We tilt our chins together, Francie and I, toward the ceiling. He shuffles his feet. I suspect that Simon is never awkward around women except when I am in the room; then he becomes adolescent.

"I'll go outside, I guess. Tidy."

When he leaves, Francie and I exchange glances. What I like most about this girl is the way we understand each other, the way our eyes talk. She picks up her hair and smoothes it into a knot. She rubs her long neck. Somewhere along the way she has put on one of Simon's sweatshirts — it bears the name of a resort we went to once — and it fits her almost perfectly. She bends her wrists and tucks her hands inside the sleeves.

"I'll check on the girls," she says. "Put them down."

"You should say 'put them to bed.' Putting down is what we do to sick animals."

She laughs and shakes her head — it's funny to her, this language of ours, the expressions, the slang. Last week, she told me there is no equivalent in German for *wedgie*, a word the children taught her.

"Tell them I'll come up in a bit." I stand and stretch, look around the spotless kitchen. "I'll go find Simon."

"Yes," she says. "You go find Simon. Good night."

Sweet girl, she comes and kisses me on the forehead before she goes loping off down the hall.

In the morning, the newspaper says that coyotes are moving down from Canada, crowded out by deforestation, urban sprawl — the usual troubles. They've been sighted on golf courses and in backyards, near fence lines, in public parks and recreational areas. The paper reports — with grisly pleasure — the list of things coyotes will eat. The adjective they select to describe this diet is *indiscriminate*. In conclusion, the article advises that small pets, children, and garbage be kept indoors at night. Finishing it, I wonder about the disasters we've been finding outside the kitchen most mornings, that I have attributed to raccoons; garbage bags we have lazily forgotten to haul out to the large plastic container, that we sling thoughtlessly outdoors to keep the dog from rooting around in them. In the mornings we find their contents scattered on the flagstone — coffee grounds and cigarette butts, apple parings and wine bottles, take-out containers eviscerated, chicken bones gnawed and strewn around.

On weekend mornings like this one, Simon wants sex. Without it he will be grumpy and easily offended; the day will be ruined. I lay the paper down on the bed and hear the house begin to come alive below us: the noise of Francie grinding beans for coffee, the girls' morning demands — cereal, fruit, chocolate, help with outfits and towels and tooth-brushing — the dog whining to be let outside. I'm jealous of her sunny carefree mornings, the simple needs of children and dogs.

After only a moment's effort, Simon rolls away and leans over me, resting on an elbow. The newspaper crinkles under his weight; I tug it free. "Concentrate," he says.

"I am," I say and squeeze my eyes shut.

I feel him tap my nose with his finger. Twice. I open my eyes. "Not on what's going on downstairs," he says. "On me."

I feel the day slipping out of my grasp. The start of the slide. I put my hands on his face and kiss him dramatically, though neither of us has brushed our teeth and both of us should.

After a moment, he pulls away. He says, "Forget it."

He sits up and fumbles for his jeans by the side of the bed. I sit up too.

"Simon," I say, "Come back." I'm sure that if I can just get him back here, inside the covers, inside me, it will all be all right. He pauses and looks over his shoulder.

"No," he says. "Not until you're interested. There's certainly nothing else wrong with you."

I lie down again. Sometimes lately, I wake up in the early morning hours and can't fall back to sleep. My mind races. My thoughts are crazy, disordered, buzzing. All over the house are dreaming beings — dogs and children and husbands and nannies — and I am wide-awake with no hope of sleeping but still not brave enough to face the dark kitchen, the insane sound of the coffee grinder at three A.M.

Simon has said, "Take some pills. I'll prescribe something." But I don't want his remedies, his pharmaceutical comforting. I can't bear to think of the noise of tablets clicking through fingers, rattling together in slim orange bottles, with their power to purge and cleanse and blur.

On her nights off, Francie goes out with her nanny friend, Katrine. I watch Simon watching them from the window; long, thoroughbred bodies folding into the secondhand cars we've given or bought them, carrying the cell phones we've distributed for emergencies, the bills we slip them above their pay because we need their loyalty and want their love. We worry about them like parents, listen anxiously for their cars and footsteps.

This morning I lie still, drifting just on the surface of sleep, and hear Simon laughing with Francie downstairs. Then the screen door bangs and there is silence. Some days, Simon and Francie take the girls to pick berries, or to some traveling carnival he's found in the paper. These are things Simon never would have done six months ago. Simon is a doctor but no longer in practice — now he's a research scientist — and he is hopeless with anything that cannot be observed in a clinical trial, aggregated and turned into a publishable article. Lately though, since Francie's come, he's gotten a tan and lost some weight; he's prone to lifting a little girl under each arm and twirling around like a top. The girls are surprised by this attention, a little wary.

The phone rings and I answer. It's my friend Sid, the one I think is involved with Simon. If I'm right, Sid falls into the category of opportunity; she is not someone Simon would go out of his way to seduce. He prefers younger women, pliable and adoring. Sid has a smoky voice and very short, stylish hair. Her appeal is in her corded muscles, her brown shoulders, and the deep laugh lines around her mouth. She has a wicked sense of humor, and I can imagine her and Simon between the sheets in some expensive hotel, emptying the minibar and saying cruel things about friends we have in common.

This morning Sid sounds cranky. She wants to know where Simon is; they are collaborating on a project together, so she has a legitimate right to keep tabs on him.

"With Francie, somewhere," I tell her. I'm torn somewhat. I love Sid and do not want Simon to hurt her — still I believe there are some boundaries civilized people don't cross. Although it may be too late for that sort of thinking. "Honestly Sid, I don't know. He huffed off a little while ago. I heard the door go. I'm still in bed."

Sid sighs. "Oh well," she says. "It can wait. Do you want to go shopping or something? Run up the credit cards?"

"I don't think so. Not today. I have to finish cleaning up from the melee yesterday."

"Oh," she says. "How did that go?"

I choose not to answer; just breathe theatrically into the phone.

"Right," says Sid. "I'll come by later then, check up."

When Sid comes, she brings gifts. Since she has always done this, even before I suspected anything with Simon, I'm not put off. Today, it's fresh bread from the French bakery and a tin of foie gras she's found somewhere. That's for Simon, of course, though Francie's eyes light up a little too. The two of them, Simon and Francie, take both these items and head outside. Simon barely nods at Sid; his kiss on her cheek is sideways, dismissive. Sid watches them go.

"Isn't that nice," she says. She starts rearranging some flowers Francie cut earlier. She positions the heads in a way she likes better, crowding them in perfectly.

"I love her," I tell Sid, a little fiercely. "She's great."

The muscles tense in her brown neck, her sharp shoulders scrunch together briefly. "I wouldn't have a stranger live in my house."

"I thought that too. But she's not a stranger anymore. The girls love her."

"Them," says Sid. "They're easy. They love *me*. Aren't you the slightest bit worried?"

She faces me across an ocean of hydrangea; hundreds of tiny stars, pinky blue, nest together in each enormous blossom.

I say, "I don't think we want to have this conversation."

She shrugs. I envy the curve of her arms, the tone and shape of them. "You knew what you were getting into."

I think she means Simon: his reputation, his travel, his appetites.

"So I did. Did you?"

I'm surprised at myself. I had no intention of saying such a thing to Sid, ever.

"Whatever are you saying, sunshine?"

"Nothing. Forget it. Tea?" I pour glasses for both of us. "Come on, we'll go keep tabs on them." I head out to the porch. I hear Sid flapping behind me, in her little thong sandals.

Coyotes are digitigrades, meaning they toe-down when they walk; you cannot see the pad of the foot in their tracks. A coyote can reach a speed of forty miles an hour when motivated.

On the phone later that night Sid says to me, "That girl's an eye-roller, did you notice?"

"Which one?" I ask. I know perfectly well whom she means. Sitting on the porch earlier, watching Simon and Francie tear at bread, sharing a bottle from the cellar, there was definitely tension.

It had rained that afternoon, quite hard, and we sat on the porch, watching it lash the trees and bend the flowers. Steam rose from the swimming pool; Simon commented on the wastefulness of heating it but made no move to step out into the wet and flip the switch. There was that silence that accompanies the fury of a good rain and the murmur of the girls quietly arguing over a board game at the other end of the porch. Over the dining room eave, the gutter was overflowing, and sheets of water poured over the windows. It looked, at moments, like water art, like a stunt you'd find in a Japanese garden, or in the lobby of a high-rise office building.

Sid said, "There'll be another leak if you don't clear that."

Francie's eyes flickered upward — a little like a racehorse, I thought — and she scraped the last of the foie gras from the tin. She was still wearing Simon's shirt; I saw Sid take note of that, register it.

Sid said, "Are you enjoying that? I'm glad."

"It's okay," said Francie. She was pulled into a ball on the couch, her knees at her eyes, a ruffle-edged pillow framing her head. Simon sat in the chair beside her; the chair was closer to the couch than usual, his knee brushed the place hers had been when we first came out, before she drew her legs up.

I said, "Francie made the best cake yesterday. Pflaumekuchen, right?"

Francie made an affirmative noise.

"It was very good," said Simon.

Sid said, "Uh-huh." She stretched out her legs and looked at the muscles in her thighs, wiggled her toes. Her thongs had little jeweled flowers between the toes; sandals are Sid's one fashion extravagance.

"Listen, Simon," Sid said then, "much fun as this is, we've got work. This piece is due in a week. We're woefully behind. We're screwed, in fact."

Sid is Simon's research assistant, in addition to whatever else they're up to. She does the grunt work, runs the numbers, checks the science. She has some degree that qualifies her for this; what it is exactly, I've forgotten.

"Oh," said Simon. "I meant to tell you. There's been an extension. We've got three weeks at least."

I may have imagined it, but I think Francie smirked. It skimmed her face like the wasp the day before, rearranged her features for an instant, and then lifted. Sid's face tried on several expressions, then smoothed again — like fresh, creamy linen swept over a dirty table.

"When did that happen?" she asked. Her voice was silky, touchable.

"I spoke to them last week, I think. They've pushed back the publication date." Simon lifted his arms and stretched them above his head; he yawned in an artificial way, one I recognize.

Francie raised her shirt and fiddled with her belly-button man.

She displayed her tongue ring, running her pink tongue through her teeth and then letting them snap on the little silver stud. My youngest girl wandered over and climbed into Francie's lap. She whispered something quite long into her ear. Francie's hair fell over Meg's face as she bent her head to listen. Then she raised her eyebrows at me and got up, took Meg by the hand, and let herself be led inside.

Sid did not watch her go; she was looking at Simon, her eyes boring a hole in his left cheekbone. I know how impervious Simon is to this sort of thing, how unaffected; Sid, clearly, hasn't yet experienced this side of him. It's like coming up against a solid block of ice; she could scrape herself bloody against it and not make a single chip.

A death certificate is just another form. Xeroxed. They come on pads sometimes, glued at the top, thick as your thumb. It's surprising to see this, the first time. It makes all that death seem incipient — too prepared for, morbidly anticipated. These forms, a dusty stethoscope, an impressive collection of first aid items, these are what remain of Simon's old medical practice. Simon lets the girls play games with these things; they like to fill out the forms for lost goldfish and hamsters. They pore over them, penciling in the blanks as accurately as they can. Name: Nibbles. Cause of Death: Trod upon. Simon signs them with a serious, official flourish.

This afternoon, my middle girl, Jodie, saw a coyote behind the house. She claims she did.

She said, "It was a dog, and then it was *not* a dog, you know?"

I asked what she would have done had it chased her, or come closer.

She gave me a serious, half-contemptuous look. "Climbed the tree, of course. I was at the tree. I said that part."

Then she asked where I'd hidden my bubble bath, the expensive kind, and after discovering its location, trudged up the stairs on her sturdy legs, with her sticking-out stomach. At the top, she stopped and turned around.

She said, "I'm doing a project for school. About coyotes. It's very educational that I got to see one."

It's been six months since Sid's husband ran off with a stripper, after emptying their bank accounts buying gaudy jewelry and trips to the Bahamas. That set some things in motion — Sid's working with Simon, for instance. Though she won't admit it, she needs the money.

Over the years Sid and I have talked about Simon — about his transgressions, my inaction. We came to a sort of silent disagreement about it; Sid would have liked me to do something dramatic: have an affair of my own, move to some squalid little apartment and get a clerical job, burn his clothes on the front grass. Those used to be her sentiments, anyway. These days she's been mum on the subject.

Back then, before Francie came, we were all in a gentle uproar. Simon was at the jittery end of some affair; Sid was experiencing those first disbelieving tremors of discovery — the rubber in the traveling toiletry case, the expanse of broad, freckled back turned on her, walling her off, night after night. My symptoms were physical, familiar, but they came this time with a pervasive sense of unease. On hills in my dreams, shadowy figures gathered and paced. I woke up every night in a sweat, my fingers pressing into my belly, catching myself in a moan or a sharp cry.

One night we drove downtown after hours; the light was disappearing behind the church steeple. The doctor Simon had sold his practice to let us in; they had redecorated the office, I noticed. Ducks and kittens frolicked in a pastel border just below the ceiling. Sid was with us; she and Simon were making jokes about my age. Miles, the doctor who'd met us there, was an old friend of ours; we'd made dinner reservations for later that night. The two of them, Simon and Miles, bent their heads over the equipment. Sid was snapping tongue depressors, making jokes. Sonogram, she said. Carrot-o-gram. Dead-o-gram. Bad-news-o-gram.

"Stop," Simon said. "Shut up."

I felt a cold, slick pressure on my belly, heard the non-noise of the machine. I looked at Sid, rolled my eyes, and grinned. But she was peering over Simon's shoulder by then, following his finger with her eyes.

Simon straightened up. He said, "Not crazy about this." *

I sat up. "What?" I said. "What's wrong?"

But he was unhooking me, freeing me from the machine. The lights dimmed. There was a sucking away as he pulled the sensor off my stomach. He and Miles huddled briefly, in that noiseless way doctors have, in the corner of the room.

Simon turned, pulled his jacket on, checked his watch. He said, "Let's go. Where are your clothes?"

"Simon," I said. "Miles. What is it?" I turned to Miles; he glanced between Simon and me and then busied himself with the machine.

He said, "Simon can explain this better. Sometimes there are complications. Age. Bad luck. It happens. We'll do dinner another time; you two should talk."

Leaving, I asked Simon questions; my voice grew shrill. He ignored me. Sid squeezed my hand on the way down the stairs.

In the car, by the aquamarine light of the dashboard, I heard him discussing this bad luck with Sid. The two of them, with their advanced degrees, spoke over my head. They traded indecipherable words and conditions. Possibilities. Responsibilities. Outcomes. I heard the word amniocentesis thrown around, heard Simon discarding it. I pulled my knees to my ears and watched streets go by the window: Main, Elm, State, Union.

Coyotes, because of their diet — indiscriminate, remember? — live remarkably healthy and long lives. Human babies are fragile things. They grow one at a time, usually. They leave your house eighteen years later, if you're lucky. Coyote pups are weaned within five days of birth. Imagine.

We kept it secret, Simon and Sid and I. Miles was on the periphery, I'm sure, pretending to advise Simon, but really, just following his orders. Simon has that effect on people; it's a quality you can easily admire from afar. I went along, even though forty miles away the city teemed with specialists, with advanced equipment and miracles of modern medicine. I couldn't think how to get there unnoticed, or how to make an appointment with a stranger. But the truth is, I didn't disagree either. I saw suddenly how much I liked my perfect children, how I had taken them for granted. What Simon suggested, and then arranged, just seemed sensible, and convenient.

We sent the girls to Simon's parents, saying we were away for the weekend. In the guest bedroom, Simon counted out a fistful of pills. They clicked together like dice. He held out a glass of water, propped pillows under my knees. Sid was there, and Simon was putting it on for both us, I could tell — being extra solicitous, trying on a bedside manner that really didn't suit him.

It was a brutally hot day, too early for that sort of weather. Around the pulled shades, angles of light intruded. Sid sat on the edge of the bed; she held a glass filled with iced tea — lemon half-moons crowded it, pushed against ice for space. Then they left me alone. I'd sleep, Simon said. Then a few cramps, like a bad period. Nothing awful, nothing dangerous.

I heard their voices as they stepped off the porch, their fading tones, the noise of their hushed laughter. The door to the balcony was cracked open for air; their voices rose and fell, alternately bright and serious.

Did I know what would happen, or am I just confusing hindsight with perception? I think now that men and women can't share that kind of secret; one sort of conspiracy breeds others. I'm thinking of people thrown together at deathbeds and in hospital corridors, at the scene of a gruesome accident — a fire, a bombing. There's a certain romance in it. It can ignite, that kind of event, lick around at whatever it finds and set the inflammable blazing.

I did drift off. When I woke, the plastic under me was sticky and hot. Their faces were there — close — lit with something other than concern. They exchanged glances.

"How do you feel?" Simon asked.

"You're sure you know what you're doing?" My voice was fuzzy, even to me.

"Trust me," he said, "I'm a doctor."

Sid giggled, then caught herself. "Shh," she said. "You'll be fine." She put her cool hand on my forehead; I smelled chlorine.

I grabbed her hand, held it there. She pulled away, slowly, said something about a cold compress.

The first cramp hit. After that it was pretty quick. The whole time — was it an hour? two? — Sid mopped around me like I was a bucket of spilled paint. Once I caught Simon staring down at me like he'd found me doing something private and humiliating.

Suddenly it was dark. I was still bleeding, but not so much. I felt faint, exhausted. I smelled gin and tonic from their glasses; the scent of a cigarette Sid had snuck away to smoke.

"Some party," I said.

Sid said, "And me in sandals." Her voice held an edge of anxiety, a little shrill, full of anticipated wrongdoing. Or so I think now.

Then I fell asleep. Vaguely, I was aware of them lifting me up, away from the mess. I heard the scrunch of plastic being balled up and pulled from under me. I felt the cool of the linen, the dampness of my hair. I pushed the washcloth — clammy, faintly disgusting — from my forehead. I didn't care what they did next.

Francie came off the plane with Simon. Why had she been in the audience at all, I asked? At a symposium about some new cancer drug? Simon didn't have a good explanation. She's here to help, he repeated, every time I asked.

I was suspicious; I moved around her like she was something dangerous and unpredictable. At first she kept to the corners of rooms, barely perched on the furniture, and said hardly a word. Watching her, though, I noticed something. She was always paying attention — to me, to the girls, to Simon. Her wide eyes followed us, gauging moods and dispositions, the potential for trouble. For such a big girl, she moved with surprising speed when it was called for, snatching Meg in midair just before she cracked her head on the coffee table. When I fainted in the kitchen, it was Francie who caught me. I woke up in her strong arms and saw her terribly blue eyes looking down at me, her features upside down.

You've had a little breakdown, Simon told me. Thorough, Sid added, but unpublicized. They were shoulder to shoulder in those days; in my mind they are always looking down on me, their eyes grave. Having me to worry about gave them another reason for conspiracy, for togetherness. They must have discussed me frequently, trading sympathetic noises and concern. I can picture Sid moving in bare feet through my house, laying a cool hand on Simon's shoulder, boiling endless kettles for iced tea, snapping mint sprigs in the herb garden.

Before Francie came, I spent sixty days curled in a corner of the wicker sofa, wearing a bathrobe. On one of them, when I wasn't paying attention, the older girls lured Meg into the deep end of the pool and held her head under water. I didn't even hear her calling for help. Correction: I mistook the noise for coyotes, far away, calling their young. The mothers cough — low guttural sounds that travel quite a distance — to warn their wandering offspring. When the sounds became human, I moved at the speed of a glacier, like I was walking through wet sand in a long dress. I stood there, pleating air with my fingers, while Jodie and then Leslie thumped Meg on the back. There was the noise of their apologies — sweet, frightened, uncharacteristic — and a retching cough coming from Meg. There were goldfinches singing and the burble of the pool filter. I watched Meg go from blue back to pink and was amazed by it.

Only a week later, they overfilled the bathtub and didn't notice until there was a full three inches on the floor. A stain like a fist opened on the kitchen ceiling, and water pinged onto the copper pots.

I see Sid come around now and perch the way that Francie did in the beginning. Empty-handed now, and unnaturally interested in the children. She is displaced and confused by the way things have changed. Simon has put off their work together indefinitely.

Francie, I have learned recently, is tremendously talented artistically. She and Jodie are working on a model of a coyote for that project at school. Last night Francie was up past midnight with modeling clay. In the morning I came down to find a likeness on the kitchen island — an intelligent forehead etched by her finger-nails, a tail remarkably bushy and exact. The face is a friendly one, but there is wariness around the eyes, a summing-up quality. Paintbrushes are stiffening in the sink; a highly sharpened pencil — for the finer work, I think — is caked with clay.

Simon and Sid had let me sleep that evening; they must have thought I would. I woke, though, when I always do, when the light is a bruise against the windows, when the house is loud with the ticking of machinery. I heard them moving around downstairs, bumping and thumping, the noise of little heels on the plank floors. I heard them louder for a moment, standing on the landing, discussing something. Simon said: Dispose of this. Sid said: Tomorrow. Put it outside. She said, Come here. He said: First, I have to . . . She said: Yes, after that.

Some mornings, even now, I know what Simon might be looking for, when he steps outside, when I hear the screen door go. He is studying the gardens for the pull of something bright and crimson across the hydrangea blossoms.

I can imagine Sid saying to him: "My God. I'm in an Australian film."

Actually, I heard her say this in the morning when they thought I was still sleeping, but their whispers had already drawn me to the window. I watched them moving around on the flagstone below me, picking up scraps of black plastic, dragging the hose through the boxwoods. In Sid's voice was some mixture of horror and delight.

I knew her so well; knew without looking that she'd be running her nails along her scalp, wearing the robe that hangs in the guest bath, the belt loose around her waist. Then she'd make coffee, after pressing her sharp features into Simon's chest.

Later that morning, when I came downstairs, the hydrangea hung heavy and sodden against the ground, as if there'd been a terrible storm. The blossoms were huge and weighted with water; they dragged the grass. Sid had cut a great many too; they dripped over the edges of bowls and vases in varying shades of blue and lilac, the merest blush of pink. Usually, it's the acidity in the soil that determines their color. I've often thought I could have true pink — the deep pink of roses and lips and blood — if I ever managed to get the balance right.

Outside in the garden it was two days before the blossoms picked themselves up again, and even then there were depressions in the grass, like heads pressed into pillows.

Men in Italy

An American woman—another tourist—
shields her eyes from the sun. Her fingers are twisted and heavy
with rings; they throw prisms against my water glass, tiny rain-
bows bursting on crystal. I sit on the terrace near the water, next
to the striped posts that mark the dock. A wooden boat approaches
from across the lake; it drifts by Queen's House, past its brick-red
facade and stacked windows, narrow and leaded.

I notice the man again. This time he's standing at the terrace
edge, wearing a dark suit and looking out at the water, which is
feathered, ruffling under a light wind. Across the lake is a child's
picture, fir trees stepping up perfectly peaked mountains. A waiter
appears and pours coffee; he smells like cinnamon and starch,

some foreign cologne. I hold the cup between my two hands, breathe in steam. I'm aware of the scent of green-tea toiletries, the ones the hotel provides in the bathrooms. I smell like green tea too, citrusy and sharp. I've bathed in it, washed my hair with it, used the soap, the lotion, the tiny perfume bottle. Every time a woman walks by, the scent mingles, strengthens.

Christina appears at the French doors; a waiter pushes one open for her, stands aside. She finds me with her eyes. I see a moment of hesitation as she searches the terrace, the way she did as a child when she'd lost me in a department store or a movie theatre. Now her face is more composed, less likely to crumple to tears, but I can still locate a trace of that childish anxiety. She walks across the terrace, soft shoes on flagstones, crisp slacks, a white shirt tied around her waist. She looks the way I wanted to seem as a young woman, efficient and pretty, tall enough to stride even in flat shoes.

"Where did you get the height?" I say to her as she sits down. In the movement of air, I smell green tea in her hair, or in mine.

She shrugs. "There he is again," she says. She points with her eyes, a trick I taught her young.

"I saw." We lean back while the waiter pours her coffee, mixes it with hot milk. She stirs in sugar, a great deal of it.

"That's four now," she says, ticking them off on her fingers. "Nice, the airport in Milan, the market in Cernobbio, here."

"I know."

We've been traveling for two weeks, a trip we planned painstakingly. Now, finally, we've landed in Como at this famous hotel. It looks just the way it did years ago, the lake, the mountains, the high ceilings of the hotel room, the formality of the furniture, the waiters, the vast dining room. Only the toiletries are different. Then, it was tuberose.

I watch the man sit down in a delicate chair, cross his legs at the ankle. I see his socks — patterned silk — definitely not American. He raises a finger and gestures to a waiter, who approaches with a silver pot of coffee. They speak rapidly; the man never looks in our direction. If it weren't for the fact that we'd seen him everywhere we've been, I'd think I was imagining that he is following us. He's never once met our eyes, never crossed a street to dodge us, done none of the things we expect from watching movies.

We saw him first in Nice. We'd been at Juan Les Pins, stuffing ourselves on croissants and glimpses of celebrities, drinking bottles of white wine, lying by the swimming pool. At night we walked to cafés, ate, and watched old men smoking and playing dice. I've taken up smoking again for the trip; it makes me feel young and reckless, tapping a cigarette into a red and blue Cinzano ashtray. Christina smokes as well; she's brought cartons of American cigarettes, but I'm fond of French ones, harsh and unfiltered, though they make me cough.

We saw him first as we walked along the beach one evening, past ice cream vendors and well-dressed tourists. He was leaning against a wall near a pharmacie, under the blue sign shaped like a cross; he was smoking. But we didn't notice him then; it was later, in Milan, when we were pulling our passports from our bags. He was talking to a girl in a dark uniform behind the Alitalia counter. I noticed him only because of the urgency in his carriage, the way he gestured loudly with his hands. I nudged Christina then, said, hey, isn't that? Didn't we see him before? But really, we thought nothing of it. Like many Americans, we think of Europe as relatively small, a series of museums and airports and train stations where you might run into anyone.

Two days ago we were in the weekend market in Cernobbio, a series of stalls strung between stone churches along cobblestone streets, selling underwear and dresses, fruit and postcards and paintings of the town. We had the string bags we'd bought; we were filling them with silly things: pencils and blood oranges and painted tiles. We were scavenging, amusing ourselves.

We stepped into the sunlight of the square; it took a moment for our eyes to adjust. In the narrow streets where the market stalls had been, the stone buildings threw dark shadows, and it was like another hour of the day entirely. We walked past the restaurants and shops toward the dock where the water taxis wait. We heard a dozen languages, spoken in pleasure and anger, disappointment and weariness. Tourists with cameras pushed past us, wearing sturdy shoes, speaking German. At a table near the edge of a café, a woman leaned across a table and threw her hands at the face of her companion, who scowled back and paid the check, slapping lire on the table one bill at a time.

Our man was standing near the dock, leaning again, and this is when I first began to think of him as a man of two postures, gesticulating and dramatic, or languid as a snake in the sun. He was studying a paper, a map, or a guidebook. He glanced up and then down again, but not quickly, not furtively. As we passed him, he turned and strolled away, back across the square toward the darkened streets of the market.

On the water taxi on the way to the hotel, where our bags had been taken earlier in the day, Christina said, "I suppose you saw him." Not really a question. I nodded. The wind was in my face; we were standing near the prow, watching the lake widen ahead of us. I could see the hotel in the distance, the battlements carved into the hillside above Queen's House. My legs remembered climbing them, the shakiness at the end of it; at the time, the view seemed scant reward.

"What do you suppose that's about?" she asked me.

"I haven't any idea," I replied. "Coincidence?"

Christina has been studying something again, pursuing another degree. It's her main pleasure and hobby, one her father encouraged: art history, anthropology, French literature. She gravitates toward mossy buildings and campuses up and down the East Coast, schools that draw girls just like her, serious girls who appreciate tweedy professors with nicotine-stained fingers — married usually; I don't ask.

This trip was my idea, to be taken during her spring break. We spoke about it on the telephone many times, poring over identical maps in our respective homes. I haven't seen Christina's latest apartment, but I imagine it to be neat and well-ordered, no milk crates or makeshift furniture for her, but full of fresh flowers and inexpensive antiques, her latest cat on a rug. I'm a dog person myself. The apartment is a brownstone on a tree-lined street; that much she's said. A landlord who likes to snoop around; she suspects him of rifling her laundry when she's at class. I don't know why she thinks this, but she's told me. Change the locks, I said, call someone. Who? she said. I didn't know, but I thought there must be someone; there's someone to call about everything these days. A bureau, an authority, a department of something or other.

But there was just silence on the other end of the phone, a change of subject, what children do to parents when they've just suggested something too foolish to merit a response. So, she said, after a pause, Rome? Milan? The Côte d'Azur?

All of them, we decided. Why not? We have some money now, I do, at least, and Christina never seems to be without — another thing I don't ask about. I love her dearly, but she has become a stranger to me — an adult woman with secrets and a life all her own. I don't recognize her clothes, her likes and dislikes. Her hair is different each time I see her. Now she is wearing it tucked behind her ears, a style I have seen lately on the covers of magazines. Also, I was astonished last week to notice she eats shellfish.

We finalized our plans over several months. I gave the dog to a friend; Christina put the cat at the vet's. We packed up our clothes, left our homes clean and ready for our return, double-locked the doors. At the moment I was locking mine behind me, I pictured her doing the same, standing on the second-floor landing in a building I imagined to be dark, a landing filled with bicycles and potted plants, doors with peepholes for screening visitors. For some reason, I imagined it smelling of Indian food, curries and tamarind. Of course, all this was silly, as there is a three-hour time difference between us. We planned to meet in New York and fly together from there.

What I could tell about Christina, from the moment I first saw her, is that she is having another disaster with a man. There's a familiar heaviness about her; she's preoccupied and laughs at things too quickly or too late. She's been going at the wine a bit too doggedly. Before the trip is out, I intend to ask her.

Now she's eating fruit, tapping a nail on a glass filled with blood-orange juice. It's the color of a sunset, or some irresistible poison.

Today we've hired a boat and a man to drive it. We're off to Bellagio; I want to see if the toy maker is still there. Christina's room when she was a girl was filled with the bright, wooden things I'd bought there: teddy bears that held little coats and pajamas, flying machines that whirred over her head as I read stories, a music box like a puppet theatre, with tiny dwarves pounding away at something, playing a tune that sounded German — or Swiss perhaps. We're that close, the border just over the mountains. We'll take a day trip later this week to Lugano, to look at jewelry, at perfectly clean streets and gardens plotted by obsessives.

"Ready?" I ask.

"Ready," she says.

As we walk across the terrace to the boat, our man is reading a newspaper. A cigarette is smoking in the ashtray near his left hand. He doesn't look up.

On the boat ride, I make the driver take us across the lake to show Christina the little town that's fastened precariously to the mountainside, the cataract that rushes furiously down, right between the houses. I point out the cypress trees, some tortured into fantastic shapes, some pruned so ruthlessly that their peaks are knife-sharp.

In Bellagio, the cafés are getting ready for lunch; waiters are flinging linen across tables, scratching the day's menus on chalkboards. I lead Christina up the twisting stone steps, steeper than I remember them, up to the town's second level. There are shops now selling glass, Murano glass and hand-blown pieces that are marvelous to look at but too delicate to imagine touching or owning. I want Christina to be charmed and delighted, and when I glance at her face, I see that she is trying to be.

"I'm fine," she says to me, preemptively.

"Here," I say and pull her into the tiny shop at the top of the steps. It's just the way I remember it, the interior dark and dusty, crowded with bright, hand-painted wooden toys and dolls, other novelties. Marionette Pinocchios hanging on hooks, wooden trains and ducks you pull along by a string. But the toy maker's added other things as well — salad bowls and servers, mortars and pestles, little wooden rings for measuring out spaghetti.

We buy things we have no use for but cannot resist: a coat hook shaped like a snail (when weight is added, the snail's head appears, smiling); another flying machine, more elaborate than the ones I had before; a music box; the marionettes. Neither of us has children to give these things to, but we want them nonetheless. While I'm paying for these — my treat, I told her — I glance around to see her staring through the front window of the shop, peering out. When she turns around, colors a little, I ask, "Our friend?"

"Who?" she says, and this strikes me as disingenuous, a false note. "No," she says, shaking her hair. "Nothing."

But she's lying, because we see him again at lunch. Over salads and mineral water, with fish on the way, I notice him sitting on a bench near the water. He has a nose like a mushroom, a dirty-looking mustache. The paper he holds is several days old; I recognize the headline from a newsstand in Cernobbio, though I have no idea what the words mean.

"Christina," I ask her, and I hear the tone that is creeping, unbidden, into my voice. "Is there something you want to tell me?"

"I don't think so," she says, pushing lettuce leaves around on her plate. She straightens the napkin on her lap. We are sitting under an umbrella. Tiny gray birds land on the pavement, peck at crumbs. I throw a heel of bread onto the ground and watch them descend, squabbling and chirping.

"That was a mistake," Christina tells me. She's right; now we're surrounded by them. One lands on the table, looks at me intelligently with black, black eyes. A waiter appears, flapping his apron, and the bird rises reluctantly, flutters away.

"Who is he?" I ask her again, when things have quieted.

Christina looks at me, then down again. "I'm not sure," she says. "I have an idea, but I'm not sure."

"Well, enlighten me," I say, playing it light, though I can't help but be chilled. What kind of man might this be, following my twenty-five-year-old daughter around Europe? What explanation can there be for this?

"Don't freak out," she says.

I can think of no response. I have never been the kind of mother who became hysterical, who overreacted. If anything, I was too self-involved, too worried about my husband's antics, less concerned about the children. Trying to unravel what lie he had told me when, which business trip was a farce, which secretary was looking at me strangely at the office Christmas party. Once, near the end, I caught him out at something and he just caved in. He told me, "It was all lies, all of it. I've never told you a true thing. Never really, not once." Well, I thought then, and think now.

"There's a man," says Christina. "One I've been seeing."

"Yes?"

"He has this wife. She's a little crazy. I think she might be having me followed."

"In Europe?" I ask reasonably. "You think she'd have you followed in Europe?"

Christina flutters her hands. It reminds me of the waiter, waving the bird off.

"Maybe. I don't know."

"Well," I say and take my napkin off my lap, fold it into thirds. "I'll ask him."

I start to stand up, but her hand is on my arm, firmly. I feel the crescent of her fingernail on my wrist. "No!" she says. "Sit down."

I do. The fish arrives; we eat in silence. The sun is warm, pleasant, and the light coming off the water is soft-edged. There is a breeze. The tables around us fill. More languages, more small dramas played out in close proximity. The café seems to me like a cluster of tiny stages where we are playing out scenes, publicly engaged in our small, private performances.

When Harry and I were first married, when Christina was very small, he had a job as an industrial psychologist. I understood that his job was to tell companies what kind of people they should hire, how they should structure their organizations, that sort of thing. He didn't talk to me about it much.

As time went on, he surrounded himself with men who owed him favors and with women who told lies glibly, smiling all the while. In time, he got richer, more important, even sought after. He was wanted to lecture at places, to consult with this company or that one. I never knew where he was, though I was always told something plausible. The itineraries I was given were universally false. I would be told he was in Lisbon, when it was likely he was in Tahiti, or Duluth. He would telephone and tell me wildly descriptive things about where he was, what he'd done, seen, eaten. All lies. He might well have been sitting in the Detroit airport describing to me camels and pyramids, exotic foods and withering heat.

Sometimes he murmured in his sleep; once he came home with the unmistakable smell of a woman in his beard.

I put up with it because it was my life; it was not what I had expected, but expectations change imperceptibly, mold themselves to circumstances.

I reconciled it as Harry's desire for attention and adoration, his need to tell you fantastic things and see you swallow them whole.

I don't know if I ever would have left him, but he saved me that decision when he had a fatal heart attack, during the one time he just happened to be where he said he was, at a hotel in Boston. A scantily clad girl may have gone dashing down the back stairs, but I don't know that and I don't dwell on it.

Now, in Italy, I do have a mind to tell Christina a few things. After lunch, we returned to the hotel, went to our separate rooms, bathed, and napped. We hadn't really spoken during the boat ride, the walk up the curving staircase, the moment when we slid ornate keys into our own tall white doors.

What could I say to her that she would heed, not brush off? All the things that occur to me seem dated, ridiculous.

Lying on the enormous bed, with a view of the lake through windows leading to the balcony, I think about this. My hair is wet, scented of green tea, and the robe the hotel has provided is too brief, giving me a clear view of my legs, which are pale, veined. These days vanity prevents me from wearing shorts. I get up and sit at the secretary, near the telephone and the stationery. I write *Dear Christina* on four separate sheets of thick notepaper. Then I outline the hotel's crest twice, in ink, and throw the sheets in the wastebasket. I light a cigarette and stand on the balcony. It's the edge of the day, and the lake is darker, colder-looking.

When Christina's father and I were here once, we danced on the terrace below. There had been a party for a hotel guest and everyone, it seemed, invited or not, drifted down, dressed for dinner. There was an enormous cake and a fireworks display at midnight, set off from a boat that appeared suddenly in the middle of the lake. We sang "Happy Birthday, Mario," in English and Italian. I never laid eyes on Mario, but we enjoyed his hospitality, drinking champagne and dancing to the small orchestra at the terrace edge. What I would tell Christina, if I could, is that life, taking its natural course, collects such dust and dirt and filth; why begin with it?

I met a girl once who told me of my own husband's intentions. She spoke urgently, self-importantly, about love and the brevity of life. Oh dear, I remember thinking, just as I thought today, when Christina spoke of this man at home, his wife.

———

At dinner, Christina is lovely, dressed in something dark and sleek. Her skin glows in the candlelight, and I want to kill the man who will hurt her. The other mothers, the ones of Harry's girls, may have felt just like this. It's a dangerous frame of mind.

"Tell me about him," I ask her over dessert.

She does. He's a dean at the university; no great surprise there. Married, nearly twice her age.

"I was pregnant," she says, "before Daddy died."

Now I am shocked. I fiddle with my knife, a thing I slapped at her for doing once, and reach for her cigarettes.

"He didn't want the abortion. He really didn't." I see in her face that she needs me to believe her, and so I do. I nod.

"He's going to leave his wife soon," she says. Now her face lights a little, but there's a candle under her chin and it may only be that. "But now, she's suspicious. She's having us followed, we think."

"I don't understand," I say. "Why would she have you followed on a trip with your mother?"

"She thinks he's going to meet me here."

Ah, I think. "Is he?"

She looks down, then around the terrace. Out at the dark water. "It depends," she says.

I realize how little I know her now. How full of calculation and arithmetic she must be. I offered this trip after her father had died, to spend some of his money, to show her something of us before it had all gone bad. But all the while, I see, she was planning something else.

I pull my sweater from the back of my chair and tie it around my shoulders. A part of me wants to hate her for this, but most of me cannot. Still, I feel ancient and ill-used. I'm suddenly aware that my arms are not taut, my hair is wiry, and my waist is thick. I have a bosom now, no breasts.

"When is he coming?"

"In two days," she tells me. "If it's all right, I'll just fly back later."

Fine, I say, that's fine.

At Harry's funeral, there were girls I didn't know. Some of them were women, some lovely, some not. All in dark clothes though, with solemn faces. They stood near the back, slightly apart. I had the impression of a grove of trees ringing the crowd, swaying slightly, slender and sad. I held the funeral at the church on the university campus, a beautiful church I have loved for years. There were lay readers and a eulogy I didn't catch the drift of, though I must have read it, approved it.

It was a bright fall day; he was to be buried in the old cemetery, behind the square. I have good friends and they held me up. Christina was there, and Jacob had flown in. I paid fleeting attention to Harry's girls, just as I had done when he lived. They were sadder than I by far, and I had a passing moment of real envy. I saw several of them, at the end, hugging one another like sisters. I might have put my own arms around them, but Christina was there, at my elbow. Instead, I held her face in my hands and put my thumbs on her cheekbones, his cheekbones, thinking a dozen things to myself, none worth saying.

Now Christina looks at me across the table. She says, "It isn't what you think. It's different."

"It's never different," I tell her. This slips out before I can find something less inflammatory.

She gets up then and I'm not surprised. I watch her walk across the terrace, step through the open French doors. In the lighted lobby of the hotel, I see her skirt delicate gold tables and chairs, step between ankles and shoulders, before she disappears behind the heavy brocade curtains.

Later, in my own room, I open a bottle of wine and sit on the balcony. There is music from below; a solitary couple dances near the water. But the dinner crowd has moved on; it's near midnight. I take my glass and sit at the secretary again, finger the notepaper, the raised lettering.

Maybe it is different, but I have no faith in it.

Early the next morning, I go downstairs and push open the doors to the terrace. At the lake's edge, the air brushes my arms. The light, barely there yet, is itself cool and silky, has a feathery touch. Bats erupt from the stone wall that borders the lake and sweep soundlessly through the sky. I pull out a wrought-iron chair and hold up my fingers. Several of them brush past, soft and fluttering. There is the sensation of fur.

This is the exact thing I did twenty-six years ago, while Harry slept upstairs; later he was annoyed to wake up and find me gone. We had an argument about it, that and why I didn't think to bring him coffee when I came upstairs. Selfish, he told me. But then, sitting on the terrace in the near dark, watching bats wheel over the lake, I was enormously happy and untroubled. It's a feeling I can't regain; I suspect it was foolish to try.

Inside, the waiters are already busy, moving quietly across the marble dining room, polishing silver, sweeping linen over tables. Eventually a waiter in a white jacket sees me through the glass and, without being asked, brings coffee and hot milk. The air is quite cool, and I resist the urge to hug myself, to quiet the chill that skips lightly down my arms, fingers the hair on my neck.

The sun appears between mountains, and within moments, as if cued, people begin to drift out the French doors. A lovely, stooped gentleman edges along the terrace with a walking stick, then the American woman with the rings, overdressed for the hour, dripping jewelry. Soon our man appears, walking along the lake path, as though he has come from town — a five-minute walk away, twenty by water taxi.

I take the letter I have written from my bag. I smooth it flat inside the envelope, run my thumbs along the edges, the creamy surface. He comes toward me and I watch him. I feel as if I am pulling him near, a little at a time. He seems like one of the marionettes I have upstairs, packed in brown paper, and I feel capable of tugging him across the flagstone.

"Good morning," I say, when he is standing across the table from me, his hands clasped behind his back. He looks curious but not concerned. He touches his mustache, brushes at it, and inclines his head.

"Good morning," he replies.

"I have this for you," I say, and I lift the envelope, hold it out. "For your employer."

"My employer?" he says. He shakes his head a little but reaches out, takes the envelope from me.

"Yes," I tell him. "The woman who is paying you."

"Ah," he says, but nothing more.

"If she's coming here," I tell him, "she'll find what she's looking for. It's all in there, in the letter."

He says nothing but slips the envelope into his jacket and tips his head. He walks away then, in the same direction, toward Queen's House and the elaborate gardens, the Romanesque statues and topiaries, the ruined battlements carved into the hillside.

I climbed these alone once. They are a medieval fantasy, turrets and staircases, secret passages and dangerously narrow walkways. At the top of them, from a stone window in the highest turret, you see the true size of the lake, stretching away, vast and calm. The trip is long, steep and arduous, one I'm not sure I could make now. Really, nothing is the way I remember it; now I recall that I made the climb after a terrible argument Harry and I had, over a dress I wanted to wear that he suddenly disapproved of. Instead of what I had hoped, that coming here would remind me of youth and happiness, it has only shown me how many wildly obvious warnings I managed not to see. Christina doesn't see them either, but there is nothing I can do about that. They are hers to ignore.

At the concierge desk, I leave the second letter with the tall man who takes and gives out room keys. I return mine. The car I have called is waiting, idling under the yellow awning, and I have plane tickets that must be exchanged. Before I turn away, I ask the concierge to tell me the story of the ballerina and the general. He bows from the waist and smiles. It is a famous story; any member of the hotel staff will tell it to you.

Many years ago, he says now, a ballerina lived alone in the

villa. While touring in Rome, she fell in love with a handsome army general and brought him home to this remote lake. But he grew restless, so far away from the bustle and industry of Rome. To keep him occupied and entertained, the ballerina commissioned these battlements that are carved into the side of the mountain. Of course, they proved ruinously expensive, and you climb them at your own risk, for now they are crumbling away in parts, as they were never intended to stand up to time. They are little more than outrageous play equipment.

Now, like then, the tall man behind the front desk bows and smiles apologetically. He says that for many years the general had played at war, at capturing flags and enemies, while the ballerina danced alone in the marble ballroom. When he finishes, he lifts his eyebrows as if to say, This may be true, or it may merely be a story to enchant guests such as yourself.

I like it still, and as the car takes me away, around the cobbled courtyard, past the gardens and shops, I turn to watch the crenellated hillside through the window, retreating, growing smaller, less imposing. I smell my hair as I turn; and for a half-moment there is the suggestion of tuberose.

The view, I remember, really was breathtaking, worth the aching calves, the bursting lungs. All around, from every angle, the lake was like something painted, the sun close and warm, the breeze from the east. The water ran with ribbons, currents, and strokes of light. Somewhere on the other side was the tiny village with the waterfall, but from that height it could only be imagined, the size of a toy you might hold in the palm of your hand. The world below merely seemed calm and bright and perfect.

Oysters

He says, "You are so beautiful. Have you read *Seabiscuit?*"

"Hmm," she says. "And yes."

They are walking down a tree-lined street. It is after dark, but just, so the light drifts away from their fingertips and butters the ends of her hair, which falls across her shoulders, brushes the corduroy of her jacket. They are going to dinner — an Indian place down the block, where amber colored lamps cast a glow on red linens and the wait staff all have honeyed voices and crisp white shirts. They'll order curries and cold beer and stuffed breads.

This, Delia thinks, is the kind of neighborhood place where a girl should be proposed to. Not that this is what she is thinking, not just yet, but someday maybe, when she can actually eat in his presence, not merely pick and push things around on her big gold-rimmed plate. In this sort of restaurant, where they will become familiar, regulars, the staff might enter into a secret plan with this man, and they would be happy to stuff her nan with a diamond. They would flutter around, peering out from the corners and from behind the bar and descend when she discovers the ring, with flashing teeth and foreign noises of pleasure and congratulation. There would be jokes about choking, and later she will think, imagine, that the ring retains the scent of cumin and potatoes.

Across the table, he holds her hand and says to her, "What am I going to do with you?"

He has a wisp of a beard, drowsy eyes, slight shoulders. He wears reading glasses; the case sits on the table between them. Sometimes he will hand them to her to clean, on the sleeve of her shirt, against her trousers. She smiles. It's a sentence so clichéd they have made it a joke between them, the kind of thing a person should never say when they really mean it.

Delia catches the eye of the waitress with the rings; they scale each of her fingers to the knuckle, delicate bands of gold in varying widths, some scrolled and scored, some simple and shining. Each time they are here, Delia tries to count them; each time she feels her number is off, ever so slightly. It's the light and the clever movement of the girl's hands, writing down their order, raising a hand to tuck a stray piece of hair back. Would the girl wear a sari to the wedding? Or when she slips off the black trousers, the starched shirt, does she become a common American woman, wearing slim jeans and a blouse, or a frothy summer dress?

Delia smiles up at her, says, "When you have a minute?"

"I love that about you," he says. "Manners. You're not pushy."

"I waited tables," she says and quickly thinks, is this new information? It's hard to remember.

"Tell me about that. I can't see it."

Delia laughs and is conscious of moving her head in a way that rearranges her hair — a woman's trick, an involuntary movement that is probably more obvious than she realizes. Everything she does around this man requires second-guessing, a review she will hold in her head at the end of the evening. What is the stupidest thing I said tonight? Did?

"I was fired almost immediately," she says. Not true, she had the job for nearly a year. But she wants the light this will cast her in: not too snobby to take the job but too refined to keep it.

"Me too," he says, "Dishwashing though. I set the record for breakage."

Delia closes her eyes. She believes him, he believes her. She is sure of this. She is unwrapping herself slowly, eking out the details, the truths, the near facts. On the other side of the table, beyond the glasses case, the dish of chutney with the tiny silver spoon, he must be doing the same. This is the best part. This and what he will do to her later, on top of her dresser and the bathroom sink and just for fun, in the bed. Then he will go home, sneaking away when she pretends to sleep, while she makes pretty, sighing noises and stretches her body in a flattering way.

He is an artist, a painter. They met at a small gallery, just around the corner from Delia's apartment. He rents studio space above it. There was an abundance of bad wine, bad art, bad breath. He had just one piece there, a massive painting she didn't understand. He found her there, teased her into conversation, let the information slip.

"Silly girl," he says to her, and his hand is on top of hers on the table. His hand is small, nearly the size of her own, and the wedding ring is a rather garish one, thicker than she is used to seeing. It seems to signal a larger-than-usual commitment. Delia removes her eyes from it, fastens them instead on his forehead.

"Aren't I?" she says, because he can't have known what she was thinking. She's light as air with this man, independent, never asking, clinging, expecting. She would never say, Stay the night, I'll make you breakfast. She has banished the word *when* from her vocabulary. When will you call? When will I see you? She clamps her mouth shut and smiles in a way she hopes is mysterious.

She places her hand over his, covering the ring but not really touching it. She makes it disappear. She says, "Curry. Red. Yellow. Green. What's your pleasure?"

The waitress arrives just then and Delia gives her an enormous smile. She pins her inside it, this young woman with her long braid, and orders for both of them, which he likes for her to do. She does it quickly, pronouncing everything correctly, with the understated air of an insider.

Stephen's wife is called Marlene. She is an artist as well, but not canvases; she paints furniture, floors, murals in people's bathrooms. Seascapes above toilets, Tuscany beyond the shower stall. He tells Delia that Marlene smells of oysters, and it sounds strangely like a compliment.

Delia is not certain that Marlene's scent is oysters exactly. Briny maybe, but to Delia the smell is quite reminiscent of plain sweat. That and oil paints; the chalky smell of gesso. Her husband, Delia's lover, on the other hand, smells of nothing at all. He is the first person she has ever met who has no scent of his own, nothing under the soap to ferret out with a gentle nose, to isolate in her head while her fingers trail across his chest, to name as pine, ocean, black currant, chocolate.

Delia found Marlene quite easily, on a flyer with fluttery bits of paper at the ends intended for tearing. It was thumbtacked on a corkboard on the way out of the co-op. It advertised interior painting, faux finishes, murals, hand-painted furniture. A photograph showed Marlene — there she was in person — leaning grandly on an old Irish linen press, now transformed, decorated with fat fruits and improbable flowers.

"Listen," Delia told her when she answered the phone, "I have a project, a job. I don't know if you're interested."

"I'm probably not. Interested." The woman sounded rushed, impatient.

"Still," said Delia, "You might be if I told you about it."

"So, go," said Marlene. She was chewing something on the other end of the phone. It sounded like twigs.

"It's a surprise," said Delia, "for my husband. I'm thinking of the bedroom, something romantic, unique."

"Sex?" said Marlene. "Is that what you're saying?"

"Maybe," said Delia, thinking about it. "Maybe." She was sitting on the edge of her bed, pleating the sheet. The apartment was chilly; the heat never worked properly. Delia always woke up with chapped red hands, her nose like she'd taken a trip in a sleigh, through snowy fields.

While she was talking, Delia walked into the bathroom and plugged the tub. She turned the water on, mostly hot, and added bubble bath. These baths warm her enough to get into bed. She likes to scald herself and then seek out the cool places between the sheets.

Marlene hates restaurants, hates food really; this is why Stephen is not afraid to frequent the Indian place with Delia, to hold her hand and lean across the table for curried kisses. The list of things that Marlene hates is long and querulous, almost deliberately eccentric. Stephen describes them at length, peeling off fingers one by one: crowds, solitude, raisins, Republicans, women who wax their legs, the English, figure skating, etc., etc. Though Marlene sounds to Delia like a pain in the rump, she sees that Stephen is charmed by her churlishness, her general disenchantment.

"Sometimes," he tells her one night in bed, while she balances a bottle of lotion in the cave of her stomach — he is rubbing her feet, — "sometimes we don't speak for days."

"That's good?" says Delia.

"I didn't say we didn't interact," says Stephen. "Just without talking."

Delia can think of no reply to this; it's too large an idea, too piercing a glimpse into their secret lives. For a moment she reviews the terrible possibilities. She kicks her feet loose from his hands and rolls onto her side; she has to fish the smooth rounded bottle from beneath her. She tosses it onto the floor, where it skitters across the hardwood and comes to rest against the metal leg of the bed frame.

"I would do anything to protect her," he says, "strange as that may seem to you."

"Hmm," says Delia. She means to sound understanding and affirming, slightly noncommittal.

"Perhaps I've said too much." Even if this is so, he doesn't sound particularly regretful.

On Delia's list of dislikes would be men who talk of other lovers, who think their lives are a fascinating bohemian romp that any woman would be interested in.

Marlene agrees. She says, "It's an arrogance, that sort of talk. They're telling you how desirable they are, how irresistible and unavailable."

"Catch me if you can," says Delia.

"Exactly." Marlene is drinking tea; she carries her own, pulled from her bag, a big hemp, hippie-looking thing, frayed and patterned like a Native American blanket. Everything she draws from this — hairbrush, bits of paper, bills, lipstick — all of it is encrusted with a sticky film, with tobacco leavings and lint. There is no other sign that Marlene actually smokes.

This is the second time Marlene has visited Delia, though no real work has begun or even been agreed to. She came in the first day like a squall, wild hair and no makeup, in a frumpy shift dress that screamed secondhand shop. She stood in the middle of Delia's studio and swung around.

She said right away, "You have a husband? Someone else lives here? I hope they're very, very small."

"I meant fiancé," said Delia.

She had wanted a look at Marlene, really; that's all. But the fact of Marlene — the busy, messy, whip-thin reality of her — was quite unexpected. Delia had to sit down. She sank onto the bed, touched the sheets that did not smell of Stephen, and rubbed her knees. Uninvited, Marlene sat too, at the opposite end of the bed, and drew her bony knees — the ugly dress had fallen aside — up to her chin. Her legs were stippled with small dark hairs; in the sunlight from the window, Delia could see the pale down on her cheeks and jaw. She thought of Stephen muttering to her, into her stomach and neck, "You. You are not a furry creature." She hadn't understood.

"Tell me about it, this painting of yours," said Marlene. She was absently fingering the faint line of hair above her lip.

"Of mine?"

"Why am I here?" said Marlene. She looked at Delia searchingly but not unkindly. "You've invited me for tea, to chat? Okay," she said and began to fish around in her bag; soon she handed Delia a fuzzed tea bag. "Lemon, if you have it." Then she stood and strode around the room. Her sandals made swishing noises against the floor.

Marlene had carried in with her a large black portfolio; she retrieved it and zipped it open on the bed. In it were pictures of her work, of rooms and floors and sticks of furniture, even the side of a barn, all covered with Marlene. Marlene's dramatic strokes, her overripe vegetation, all of it at odds with this Marlene who occupied Delia's apartment, who seemed the type of woman to paint slashing abstracts, or people with missing pieces and faces like jigsaw puzzles.

"I know what you're thinking," she said. "Don't say it. It's not me. But I'm the breadwinner of the house. He's the artist." She gave this last word a dripping sort of verbal italics. The word hung, shimmered, twanged a little in the room.

Delia's apartment captures the light from wide windows on three sides, old-fashioned windows that either stubbornly stick or crash down unexpectedly. Once one shattered in the middle of the night, making her scream out loud. The furniture is unfinished, mostly pine, spare of line and interest: a low bed, a dresser, a relatively good couch inherited from a friend who had gotten married, few knickknacks or photographs. Decorating is something she has meant to get around to but hasn't.

She told Marlene she wanted to warm the place up a bit.

"I didn't want to mention it," said Marlene. "But it is a little monk-y." For a moment Delia wasn't sure what she meant.

Delia imagines Marlene and Stephen living in fantastic disarray, with toppling stacks of books and candles melted into the floors and splatters of paint thrown about like gore from some horrific murder. But this is all in her mind; she doesn't even know where they live exactly. Stephen references the bottom floor of some many-roofed Victorian monster on the other side of town, talks disparagingly about their landlord's attitude toward routine upkeep, and complains about the dangerous moodiness of the pilot light. Other than that, nothing.

When Marlene leaves, Delia realizes they have discussed nothing of consequence. But when she returns the next day, she is friendly, talkative, almost sisterly.

"I've been thinking about you," is what she says when Delia answers the door, after she has marched in and sat herself down on the rumpled bed.

It is Saturday morning, and Delia has not heard from Stephen for two days. She was not expecting Marlene. Instead she has been watching out the window, through the lace curtain that was here when she moved in, half-expecting to see Stephen's bouncy little figure appear around the corner, his long coat blowing around his ankles, the private, demonstrative little movements he makes with his hands even when he is alone. She has told him that he looks like a crazy street person, someone you would give a wide berth to. Good, was his reply.

Now Marlene rifles her bag and pulls out a folded sheet of paper. When she opens it, she reveals a startlingly good likeness of Delia. In the sketch Delia is lying down, her face turned, her lips parted. She looks a bit transported, more romantic than she is in real life. Is it Botticelli she's reminded of? Perhaps. The loose hair, the rounded softness, the slight otherworldliness to the eyes. The nudity. But that's not all. Entwined with Delia, this idea of Delia, is another figure, one not unlike the chalk outline of a body, the kind seen in film noir, below a naked swinging lightbulb. Hollow arms enclose her; one vacant leg drapes hers. A penis, rigid with nothing, rests against her thigh.

Marlene apologizes. "It's weird, I know," she says, "But I wanted to get something down. I was watching you yesterday. I think I know just what you look like making love. So I dashed it off. Am I right?"

Delia smooths the paper on her knees. "I don't think I have any idea."

"Right," says Marlene. "But you should. Look like this, that is. It's my idea of it. My interpretation."

"Listen," says Delia, "I might be wasting your time here. Probably I am."

"Did you break up with him?" Marlene lies backward on the bed with a comfortable familiarity, as though they have been friends for years and have a treasury of confidences between them.

"I don't know you," Delia tells her.

"So? I'm here. You can tell me about how he cheats on you and leaves the cap off the toothpaste and comes too soon and has boorish friends, eats rare meat, doesn't walk his dog enough. Does he steal silverware, have mossy teeth, support the missile defense shield? Tell me all of it, I'm listening."

Delia studies the paper with her likeness. She looks like the kind of woman to whom none of these things should happen, or be possible. She looks disastrously beautiful.

She says to Marlene, "You don't wear a wedding ring."

Marlene looks down at her hand, surprised. "Why would I?" she says. "I'm not married."

On another evening with margarine light, a deep, scorching yellow, Delia searches for Stephen's hand with hers. They have come clattering down the stairs of her apartment and pushed open the door into the street. The long line of row houses is quiet; the river glints in the distance, flashes of it visible through the maples and elms. Delia would like to walk down the towpath with him, beside the old barge canal on the pale, pebbled path. Here, people push strollers and lead dogs, wander with hips pressed together and faces turned into each other's jackets. She'd like to walk down to the wing dam, jutting into the center of the river; when the water is low you can step out and walk its peaked ridge with water lapping at your shoes. You wind up in the middle of the river, the old mill on the opposite shore and the roughest part of the river running and tumbling around your feet. Stephen won't go there though; it's too public.

In the Indian restaurant, the girl with the ringed fingers flutters a glittering hand at them, waves them to seat themselves. They are regulars now. Their beers appear almost instantly; the bread will follow unordered.

"Tell me about your wedding," says Delia.

"I barely remember it," says Stephen. He is studying his

glasses for smudges, holding them up to the light and turning them back and forth. Sitar music stutters and then rises, quivering like something you could pluck with your fingers. Someone adjusts the volume.

"But you must." Her voice is teasing, uncomplicated. "I promise not to be jealous."

In her apartment, where they have just spent another unscented afternoon, a drape of scarlet velvet has been hung on the wall behind the bed. It hangs from an iron rod that Delia found in the back of the broom closet in the kitchen; the fabric itself came from a flea market. She had bought it months ago with the thought of draping it across her bed. She had been thinking it would give the place the feel of a harem, something rich, reminiscent of Constantinople. Instead it just showed up the dullness of the studio — it was stark as a cell. Now it hides the beginnings of this new Delia, this naked languid woman whose curves are more generous than her own and in whose mouth and lidded eyes Marlene has combined promise and denial.

"It's not important," says Stephen, "Why torture yourself?" He plays with the bread, tearing it thoughtfully, slipping small pieces into his mouth. Of the draped curtain he has said nothing.

"Humor me," she says. The beer bottle is cold, but inside her humid palm it quickly grows warm. She is ready for the truth, both expectant and unhopeful. She stares at his ring, which he twists, taps against the edge of the table. The sound is muffled, smothered by linen.

In her bed alone, under the velvet backdrop, Delia has considered the contradictions and their possible meanings. He isn't married, he is. He is lying, Marlene is. He is merely testing her commitment. He is a scoundrel using this fabricated marriage as an excuse to keep himself free of entanglement.

"Sometimes it's not even conscious," Marlene had said that afternoon. "You'll notice suddenly that you're doing things yourself, completely separately. Like the bed. I bought a bed last week by myself, without any consultation. In the back of my mind I was thinking, well, I can always take this with me because it's mine, free and clear." Marlene paused. "Take you, for instance. You live alone. You have this mysterious fiancé; there's no sign of him at all, not even that man smell. And I wonder, is this an accident? Have you already gotten rid of him?"

These afternoons with Marlene, over shared mugs of tea, made from the grubby bags that she totes around, have taken on a strange significance for Delia. Yesterday Delia agreed, or discovered, that she does not care for raisins either.

"It's the surprise raisin that bothers me," said Marlene. "If I'm expecting it, it's okay. But to suddenly bite into one where I wasn't thinking one would be — that really frosts me."

Now Marlene drags things with her into the apartment: three-legged stools that she is turning into fairy-tale mushrooms, a rocking chair she is repainting in a shocking plaid. Delia has had some trouble keeping her away from her own furniture. Often Marlene will hover over something with a brush in one hand, waving it around, touching her tongue to her upper lip.

To distract her, Delia turns the conversation to other things, Stephen in particular. Marlene rarely uses his name. Him, she calls him. Whatshisname. On Marlene's list of dislikes, Stephen seems to be in rapid ascent. Delia is quite certain that Marlene intends to break with him. Delia's plans, never fully formed, are now under revision. She had thought early on of having Marlene paint Stephen on the wall, wrapped around her. Once the body was in place she'd spring the face on Marlene, stand back, and see what sort of a smash up that instigated.

Now she thinks, hang on there. Better to let Marlene do the dirty work, be there to pick up the pieces.

"All right," says Stephen, finally. "If you really want to know. We got married in a church, believe it or not. One of those hard-core gospel churches with a fire-and-brimstone preacher and hammy-armed women swooning in the aisles. Then we were dunked in a river while the choir sang 'Old Time Religion.'"

"You're making that up," says Delia.

"There were lots of big hats and people fanning themselves with palms. They advertised a funeral home on one side, roadside barbecue on the other."

"Liar."

"Maybe," he says. "Suffice it to say, it was lovely."

"I wonder sometimes if you're married at all." Between them, the food steams. In a blue and white enamel bowl, a mound of rice rises, gentle as a knoll.

His expression doesn't change. He blinks at her and folds his glasses neatly, snaps them into their hard case. "Why would it matter? We're friends, right?"

Friends. It's one of his favorite words. He likes the carapace of it, the deceptively protective connotation. He said to her in the beginning, We'll be friends of course? Good, good friends.

She hadn't minded it then; it had seemed adult and sophisticated, a little arch, the kind of word that can be said deliberately, stuffed with meaning, or can just as easily be crumpled and thrown away. A garbage word, full of nothing.

When they come out of the restaurant, the street is dark. In the distance the white spire of the church is lit, piercing a thick sky. He swings their hands together between them. A frivolous connection. It is not at all like lovers holding hands. She thinks about the things he does, the way he absents himself from their lovemaking, the mechanical movements of his body, the way he can rescue a moment from tenderness by a sudden playful gesture, blowing wetly into her ear or navel, whispering some nonsense.

"He's too serious," is what Marlene has said. "Oversentimental, anxious. It makes me insane. Sometimes a girl just wants to get laid, follow?"

While she was saying this, she was painting. The sound of her voice was at odds with her hands, moving in quick, hummingbird strokes, painting wisps of hair around Delia's face. She has outlined, in charcoal pencil, the figure of the man making love to Delia. The man, the body, is large and anonymous but grandly sexual.

"This is what I need," said Marlene. "This guy," she ran the edge of her brush along the figure's inner thigh, lightly touched its penis. "Mr. Right."

"Would he ever cheat on you?" asked Delia.

Marlene laughed. Not a self-satisfied, full-of-cream laugh, the kind of a woman too stupid or smug to entertain the possibility, but one of a woman not at all concerned, one who would not view this sort of thing as a disaster, or even an event. Delia thinks of Stephen saying, I don't have a jealous bone in my body. Nor does Marlene.

In these words Delia hears more fatalism than hipness. Delia sees Stephen and Marlene as riders on runaway horses, or passengers in a car driven by a madman. They have the kind of control gained only by giving it up entirely, as if they can see the bridge abutment coming at them through the windshield and with horrified detachment say, Well, there's nothing I can do about this.

"Not in any way that matters," Marlene said and went on painting. The figure on the wall is in danger of becoming as obscene as any fertility god; it has a huge, threatening sexuality.

"I won't be able to sleep under that," Delia told her.

"You'd like Stephen. You should meet. I should set you up." Marlene wore cutoff shorts and a tank top patterned like the henna dyes Indian women paint their bodies with. Delia has noticed these lately on the wrists of the girl at the restaurant, where they protrude from her cuffs. She might be covered head to toe with such snaky designs, from collarbone to ankle. Mehndi, Delia remembers.

"I may not be kidding," Marlene said and turned to look at Delia. "I'm moving out soon. Me and my bed. This fiancé of yours is history; you haven't said but I can tell. One self-centered artist, capable of gestures both grand and insincere, going cheap."

"Thanks, no," said Delia.

Suddenly, this Stephen of Marlene's is not one she wants after all. Not in the daytime, with the dust-freckled light coming through the windows, bouncing off the hardwood floors, showing both their faces in an unforgiving clarity. He seems a cast-off, something Marlene has pulled from her bag and held up for scrutiny, an item tainted by Marlene's brutal disinterest and sticky with use.

When Marlene leaves, or when Delia does, for now she has grown used to having Marlene in her apartment even when she isn't there, they kiss solemnly. Marlene bends — she is quite tall — and touches Delia's mouth with hers. It is a sweet, inconsequential intimacy, and beneath the rampant sex of the figures on the wall, it seems a perfect innocence.

These days, the phone is always unplugged. She has told Stephen that there is some problem in the line, its connection to the street. He does not seem worried. He appears in the evenings, often quite late, with his customary rap on the door, more a blow than a knock. In her bed, she touches his hollow limbs and his unscented neck and floats away. It is a parody of love, their coupling, and Delia's heart retracts accordingly, while her fingers become stern and practiced. She arouses him in all the predictable ways, joylessly, but with a certain superior detachment that is not without its own pleasure.

"Something's changed," he tells her. "You're different, more passionate."

"I'm going to find a real boyfriend or lover soon," Delia says to him. She rolls away, her skin skittery on her bones; her hands search for coolness, for the unexplored undersides of pillows.

"That's a good idea," he says. In the dark he turns to her and whispers, "I'm afraid of you, of how I feel. We need to stay sane about this. Be grown-up. I'm scared of what might happen."

Delia thinks, I could kill you quite easily. She stretches the muscles in her legs and reaches out her hands to touch the stuccoed walls behind the drape — the feel is like the rind of melons. She thinks of Marlene saying, I wish he would disappear. You should be able to paint lovers over when you tire of them. Just gesso them away, like a flower you thought would resemble O'Keeffe, but instead just looks like a cunt.

Marlene's intrusion into Delia's apartment is slow but steady. A tin of the strange tea she drinks takes up residence on the kitchen counter, paintbrushes fill the ceramic toothbrush holder in the tiny bathroom, her thick-bodied candles melt into artistic puddles on the nightstand. Delia notices one day, coming inside, that there is a scent about the place that is new and unfamiliar — the smell of another body, another person's life and detritus; an odor she has missed without quite realizing it.

"Are you going to help me move this bed of mine?" Marlene asks one chilly spring afternoon. They are walking along the towpath toward the wing dam. On one side is the murky canal, on the other the tumbling river. A few kayakers are out in the rapids, beating against the current. A loosed dog rushes between them; Marlene reaches down to touch it and comes up with hands covered with white fur. She brushes them clean on Delia's sleeve.

"Sure," says Delia. "Whenever you want."

"Now's good," Marlene says. "How about now?"

The bed is not so much a bed but a headboard and footboard. A rickety brass antique with little round balls that move back and forth like those on an abacus. They carry it easily enough, one piece at a time, all the way across town. It takes two trips, one for each piece. The weekend crowds are out — the tourists and antique collectors, the art lovers, young families and couples in search of quaint.

"This town," Marlene says, "is getting discovered. We should drive upriver on the weekends, run for it."

Delia had been thinking the same thing. She and Stephen had discussed it once or twice, but it came to nothing. The house where Marlene took her to retrieve the bed was not what Delia expected, outside of being vaguely Victorian. It had been cut up into small apartments, and the one thing Delia recognized as belonging to Stephen was that overlong topcoat, tossed across a bar stool. Otherwise the apartment had only the normal trappings of shared domestic life — common magazines on a low table, stained coffee cups, half-empty bookshelves, a bed covered in patchwork quilts — a bed that had been thrashed around in, from the look of it, with mismatched sheets and flattened pillows. They left the mattress on the floor, pulling from it the linens Marlene claimed were hers. They left just one pillowcase and a torn, hand-knitted afghan.

Delia was surprised that it moved her not at all: this bed, this apartment, that coat of Stephen's, the pockets of which might still contain some trace of Delia — coins she had lent him for laundry, a mint from the Indian restaurant.

She had not even wondered, more than fleetingly, if they might run into him. Of the look that would cross his face if they met on the stairs, of the strange picture she and Marlene made twisting the unwieldy bed frame over the landing, pillowcases tucked into the back pockets of their jeans.

"Won't you tell him?" asked Delia, looking around the apartment from the doorway on their last trip.

"He'll figure it out, I think," said Marlene.

Halfway down the street, stepping around a baby stroller, she said, "The truth is, he knows already. He's got someone else. I may have been less than honest about that part. I can stay with you for a while — that's okay, right?"

"Yes," said Delia. "Yes, of course."

The headboard they lean against Delia's wall behind her bed. The finials just reach the bottom of Marlene's painting, and Delia wonders — for a half-second — how the measurements could have been so exact. Marlene makes the footboard a grate in front of the nonworking fireplace.

At the Indian restaurant some days later, Marlene touches Delia's hands across the table. Lightly. The Indian girl puts bread in front of them, and Marlene touches her slim fingers as they pass by. "So many rings," she says. "Look, we don't have any." She takes Delia's hands and turns them up for inspection, with her own.

The girl smiles shyly and pulls the sleeve of her blouse up to the elbow. Bracelets of henna circle her arms, one above the other, as intricate as the gold she wears on her hands.

Above the bed, Marlene imitates these patterns on Delia's body. She paints her ringed with blue and indigo, snakes swallow each other on her arms, thick bands of green circle her lazy thighs, one turned ankle.

The man's empty figure, featureless as well water, regards this blankly. Lying under Marlene's scrutiny, Delia smells paint and lemon tea and, distantly, a smell like that of an oyster bar in the open air, by a blue sea.

Collected Stories

In the early evenings, Ella and Victor hang around the porch, gardening or chatting, reading novels and newspapers. It's late August and the perennials are in second shift, phlox fading and andromeda edging in. The roses that edge the porch, scrolling the columns and eaves, have sprung dark red leaves, promising a last blazing riot. Soon Victor will need to unearth burlap from the garage, lay it down over the roots, and take down the awnings. The time is coming to move indoors, lay in firewood.

In these final, glowing summer evenings, they wait, talking of this and that, for the hour when they can break out all their vices: the cocktails, the cigarettes, the way they speak to each other when they are a little drunk. Come six o'clock they will start to blur the edges, sand the day down to something smoother, more manageable.

For Ella, this waiting gives the hour a feeling of restraint, a civilized kind of deprivation. At some point later, a decision will have to be made; will they end the evening in an argument or console each other with talk of love, their good life? But now, everything is pleasant, promising. They speak of Victor's children, they remind one another of when school begins again, and they argue about the dog's weight. Victor is convinced the dog is fat; Ella cannot bring herself to stop feeding him.

Ella is happiest when Victor is kissing the dog or playing games with him in the swimming pool. Victor wants the dog ten pounds slimmer, and he wants to be alone in bed with Ella; the hair rises on his neck when he feels her pat the bed, calling him up. They make love next to this enormous animal, who sleeps, and sometimes snores, throughout.

"I never thought," Victor tells her, "that I'd be doing this with a dog."

This is the point at which Ella may or may not bring up Victor's ex-wife. Living with Victor gives Ella much of what she needs, in terms of security and advantages. It is to Ella's benefit that Victor has three children who need mothering on the weekends; it puts him in her debt, a place she likes him. Used goods, she likes to call him. Shopworn.

Victor's ex-wife either teeters on the brink of suicide or is manically upbeat, depending on chemical intake. "Why won't she just get on with it?" Ella will say after the fourth call in as many hours. She will offer to buy the Drano. But her suicide is not really what Ella wants. Victor's ex-wife is a fixture in the stories she tells her friends. (The ex-wife asked Victor, Do I need to tell the new German au pair that the children are half-Jewish? After all, you do remember what happened. . . . This, Ella told this morning, to her friend Liz.)

Every morning Ella and Liz walk dogs. They make long, looping circles through the woods and tell each other their complaints. Liz talks about her husband, Daniel; Ella makes up stories about Victor. There's nothing really wrong with Victor — that's the trouble. Ella met Victor at the last job she had; now he has another and she doesn't have one at all. Victor loves Ella in a way that makes her feel tired, vacuumed out. Her disinterest is her failing, she thinks. Every morning she wakes up and vows to do better, to not criticize the smallest things he does: how he drives a car, the way he turns down the radio before making a sharp turn. Every evening she's back on the porch, smelling roses and mint, aware of the trace of chlorine in her hair and about her shoulders, tuned to the sound of the day ticking slowly toward six o'clock.

The porch where she sits is wide and wraps around half the house; it looks over the swimming pool and the rose garden. These features are what Ella and Victor admired when they chose the house. The furniture on the porch they bought, right down to the knickknacks, from the previous owners. The roses and the English gardens endeared the house to them; now they can't imagine how to keep up with it all. A parade of gardeners and landscapers have pointed out Japanese beetles and black spot, dead birches, and an unidentified disease on the dwarf Alberta spruces by the front door.

This evening, Victor is somewhere in the garden while Ella lounges on the porch, reading. She has raccoon-eyes from swimming; she wears one of Victor's T-shirts, hanging to her thighs, a bathing suit underneath.

"Victor," she says. "Where are you?"

There is no reply. She looks around until she sees smoke rising from a rose trellis behind the cypress tree, to the left of where she sits. She walks over.

"Do you know how I found you?" she says. "Roses don't smoke, generally."

"No?" he says. Victor is pruning roses; by his feet is a pile of clippings. He holds curved shears in his hand. He drops his cigarette. Ella picks it up. For all of Victor's organization, his fascination, for instance, with desk accessories and rearranging them, he has small, piggish tendencies. He drops cigarette ends and ice cream wrappers; he shells nuts on the counter. Ella, on the other hand, lets clothes fall where they come off — genuinely does not see the trail she leaves from one room to another — but still she hates dirt, trashiness.

"Do you know," she says, "What Liz told me today? Once, when she and Daniel were first together, after a romantic dinner, he sat her down on the couch and asked her what her grade point average was. And then what, if any, operations she had ever had."

"Dare I ask what you said about me?"

"The usual," she says. "Do you want tonic or soda?"

"Soda, if we have it. Did I say that my family is coming, on Sunday?"

"I don't believe so," she says. "But thanks for the notice."

In the house, she mixes drinks, takes her cigarettes from the cabinet. She considers checking the answering machine, but since she has no intention of returning the calls, she walks outside again and hands Victor his glass.

Later, relaxed and drowsy, they discuss the dog. Ella likes to talk about him, whether or not they should get another (not until the cats go, says Victor, who is violently allergic), whether those bites of his might be fleas, and while we're on the subject, why does he bite people for no good reason? They are thinking of the previous week, when he had bitten Victor's boss without any provocation. This man had stopped over with a housewarming gift.

"He put his face too close," says Ella.

"Don't make excuses," says Victor, who has been apologizing for four days, avoiding looking at the crescent bruise under this man's eye. The story has now swept through his office and he is the butt of a number of jokes; it's not a position he appreciates. Nor does he care for Ella's general indifference on the subject. Victor remembers this as though it had happened moments ago, the dog leaping, the growl and snap of jaws, and the remarkably, absurdly small mark left there, which swelled and reddened as they stood near the rose trellis, stunned and horrified.

"He took it well, I thought," says Ella now.

"He was gracious. It's not the same thing."

Victor looks at Ella. She hasn't changed clothes, and she sits with her legs drawn up, showing him her pale legs, the darkness between them. Her hair is pulled back in a way he dislikes; she is prettier with it loose. While he looks at her, he thinks about his daughters. They are surprising him lately, with their beauty, their slimness, the look of their skin; the way they tell him jokes that are actually funny; the way the oldest cheats shamelessly at cards. He is surprised, too, by the rush he sometimes feels around them, the intense feeling of pride and fear. He is fearful about what is coming; he dreads boys on motorcycles and orchid corsages and round plastic containers of pink pills. Ella likes to tease him, to elaborate the wild ride ahead. She manages to hold herself at a distance, as though she is a bystander, merely observing. It annoys Victor, her separateness, the way she refuses to interfere or participate.

Probably it is this reluctance that makes him determined to drag motherliness out of her. He thinks it can be extracted, lured into the open. He wants to make her pregnant, see her lumbering around the house, swelling out clothes. He likes the idea of her breasts in this state. He would feed her cravings, elevate her feet, sing to her stomach.

"Come here," he says now. "Let's make a baby."

Ella doesn't move. She snorts. It is a joke and it is not a joke; Ella knows this. Right now, she is thinking about the boy who has been working at the house, painting, tearing down the dreadful wallpaper that covered every visible surface. Ceilings, even. His name is Rolan, and in the evenings she likes to think about him.

He comes from Mexico; he is the youngest of ten, he told her. Ten children? she had said, astonished. Ten *boys*, he told her. All day, while Victor is at work, Ella and Rolan are alone in the house. There is a shy sweetness about Rolan that Ella finds irresistible. He has a puppy's worried expression, the gold-edged eyes of an Aztec.

She makes him lunch, ferries him bottles of water. He tells her about where he comes from, about how he and his brothers swam in the river every day, drank from it, washed their clothes. He tells her this sitting on the porch over cartons of bad Chinese food, looking over the swimming pool. How old are you? she asked him today. Twenty, he said. I remember twenty, she told him. You could swim, she said then, a little too quickly, to fill the space that had become suddenly taut with the idea of her age. Rolan only ducked his head, showed her his pale neck.

At night she dreams about him in a river that looks like the swimming pool, the same blue, the same ripples that skip across the surface. A river bordered by flagstone and banked by peonies, frowsy, shaggy-headed peonies, planted in stripes of peppermint and cream. She sees him porpoise through the water, his thin arched back, the water running off his short, short hair. She can see the shape of his skull underneath. But she can't see his legs, can't imagine that part of him.

Victor says it again, "Come here." He opens his arms.

This is the moment; right here. Where will they take it? Ella sees two choices, possibly three. They shimmer there for a moment, in the citronella-scented air. The sound of crickets rises from the dark gardens, fills her ears.

"I'm going to bed," she says and stands up. She leaves her glass on the floor but picks up the ashtray, takes it to the kitchen and empties it. The dog opens one eye and gets to his feet, slowly. He follows Ella into the house.

Victor stays outside. They've skipped dinner again, which doesn't seem to bother Ella at all. When he first fell in love with Ella, he was married. He got his divorce to be with her, a thing he believes she should appreciate more than she does. He lost his job and was fortunate to get another one. The divorce and its aftermath were hellishly expensive; now he has bought Ella this house she wanted. The cost of gardening alone could send him to the poorhouse.

Liz has had a cold for two weeks; it has gone on so long that Ella forgets to ask about it. Ella herself never gets sick. This worries her. She assumes that the universe is holding something much worse in store for her, waiting for her to get complacent, to begin saying, "I *never* get sick." She keeps her mouth shut. This gloominess she drags around with her is something she attributes to the death of her parents, one right after the other, just before her thirtieth birthday. Her parents spent three months locked in a death race; she remembers driving from hospital to hospital, certain that she would be at the wrong one at the critical moment. Now she feels like a marked woman, and so she drinks and smokes and thinks herself brave and reckless and stupid.

"You should see a doctor," she told Liz that morning.

Liz said, "I hate doctors. I don't want to go unless I'm bleeding from my ears."

Last week, Victor told Ella about a man in his office who went to the doctor, complaining of being tired. He was dead and buried in less than four weeks. Victor, relating this, sounded thrilled and horrified. A liver ailment. Incurable.

"Suppose he hadn't gone to the doctor," Ella said to him. "Would he still be here?"

"Maybe," Victor said. "Probably not."

"I bet he would. Knowing did him in."

Ella said this lightly, but she half-believes it. She can't shake the feeling that that there is more safety in ignorance than actual bliss. She thinks of those people you hear about, the ones who are diagnosed with cancer but refuse treatment, return to their homes to compose and prepare themselves, but then, against all odds, become well again, return to their jobs, raise their children, shop at the supermarket.

Last winter, before they had moved, Victor's grandmother had broken her hip. (It's so trite, Victor had said, her *hip*.) They had gone to visit her at the hospital one frigid evening. She had a semiprivate room in a place that was half hospital, half nursing home. Victor made the mistake of taking Ella through the nursing home, the quicker way, but it sucked the breath right out of her: all those slumped figures in dressing gowns, sitting in wheelchairs right in the middle of hallways, as though they had wheeled themselves halfway and then given up, or worse, as though someone pushing had just left off and marooned them, leaving them staring into space or at their own wasted knees.

Victor's grandmother was nearly ninety-five. Ella had never known such an old person before and was surprised when they first met to find her sharp and fully functioning. (All systems go, Ella said to Victor later. My people start to decline at about age thirty-five.) But that night in the hospital, immobilized under tissue-thin blankets, Celia seemed weak and a little grotesque. She was worried about her hair—waist-length, textured like a horse's tail. She complained about how undressed she felt without anyone to put it up for her. Just then, it was fashioned into a loose, untidy braid that disappeared under her shoulder.

"I could try," Ella offered, praying that this would be refused. Celia ignored her.

The rest of the visit was spent talking about the kinds of things Ella particularly does not like talking about—intestinal matters.

Ella thinks of secret machines churning away inside the body, doing what they are supposed to do, while no one discusses them.

At some point the conversation veered off. Victor was asking about Celia's childhood, her memories. She said over and over again, "I've had a hard life. I've had a terrible life."

Victor pressed on. He wanted to hear this story and that one. How she met his grandfather (they were first cousins, Ella knew; that they met is not magical or serendipitous); the farm she grew up on, the cows she milked, the fields she plowed, behind driving horses. And so on. She married at fourteen, had six children before twenty-one.

Ella thought, it does sound rotten. She was standing near the window, fingering the heavy industrial-weight curtain. Every ten minutes or so, an enormous whooshing noise could be heard, the kind of noise that shakes things — a freight train careening through below. There was no light from it, just the horrendous sound.

"How can you stand this?" Ella asked. "This noise?"

"What?" said Celia. "Oh, it doesn't bother me."

She went on. "It was terrible, my life. I had no childhood. I was in charge of looking after all the children. I was a mother before I was a mother. I was a mother to my sisters and my brothers."

Finally, mercifully, a woman came around and made them leave. They stopped for take-out food on the way home. Ella asked Victor, "Why did you make her go on like that, talking about those things? It's miserable."

"Old people like that," Victor told her. "They like to talk about the past."

"What makes you think that? Maybe they don't. I wouldn't."

"They do, though. They like to remember things."

"I think it's you that likes it. Dragging out all her horrible old memories and collecting them like a rag-and-bone man so one day you can tell your children: she worked on a farm, she whacked the heads off chickens. You're antiquing through her head. I bet you never asked her anything before you thought she was going to die."

They didn't speak after that. Ella didn't go the hospital again. Victor went alone, after work. He came home and told her that his grandmother asked after her. She nodded but was immovable. Victor had thought, she's like the dog when she makes that sort of decision. He was thinking of when the dog is sleeping; he becomes so inert and heavy you can barely lift his head off your lap to get up.

When she knows Victor's family is coming, Ella makes sure to invite Liz for the afternoon. It takes the edge off, gives her someone to disappear into the kitchen with, make fun with. Liz brings some little things she's picked up: shelled shrimp, a loaf of bread, hummus. They are arranging them in the kitchen.

Victor comes in and says, "Keep those away from my grandmother, she's kosher."

"Keep what?" says Ella, and then Liz, nearly together.

"Shellfish." Victor lights a cigarette and smokes it by the window, blowing through the screen.

Celia is better now, but frail; she's sitting in a wheelchair on the porch with Victor's parents, his daughters. The two oldest girls are having an argument about ice cream; it has been going on nearly an hour.

Ella tells Liz, "There's one ice-cream bar with nuts, one without. They'd rather argue about who gets which than actually eat the damn ice cream."

"Which is more valuable?" asks Liz. She is slicing a lemon and coughing into her hand; perfect spoked circles fall away from the knife.

"The plain one, apparently."

Victor says, "I'm proposing some sort of triathlon — running, swimming, and taking food away from the dog. Whoever survives gets the choice ice cream."

"Speaking of," says Ella, "Let's not leave him alone with your broken, Scotch-taped-back-together grandmother."

"Good thinking," says Victor and scoots out of the kitchen. Ella picks up his cigarette and finishes it.

"You're good to put up with all this," says Liz.

"Aren't I?" says Ella. "Aren't I a brick?"

On the porch, Victor is telling the girls one of his grandmother's stories. It's his favorite, and Ella glances over. There's Celia in the wheelchair, knotty hands twisted together in her lap, the old-fashioned shirtwaist dress, hair now wrapped so tightly around her head you'd never know it reached her waist; it hasn't been cut since she was a girl. Her eyes are closed.

"When Bubby had her babies," he is saying, "she had them upstairs in the bedroom, while Grandpa sat downstairs in the kitchen and read the paper. Her mother came over and she had the baby, and then Bubby got up and went downstairs and cooked him dinner."

Liz smiles and eats a shrimp. The girls seem skeptical; probably they are just thinking about ice cream.

"Isn't that right?" says Victor. He looks at his grandmother; Ella looks too. Celia opens one eye at a time and smiles at him. It's a small smile, an indulgent one.

"I made him a pot roast," she says slowly, "with carrots and root vegetables."

"See?" says Victor. His voice is a little shout. "Just as I said."

The girls return to the ice-cream wars. Victor's father has fallen asleep at the edge of the wicker sofa. His mother is rubbing lotion on her knees; her legs are heavy, like a fallen cake, patterned with veins the exact color of blueberries.

Now Celia says something else, but in Yiddish, and Ella and Liz look at each other. Victor's mother responds, and this conversation continues for several minutes. Victor looks away. Liz sneezes. Ella gets up and clears plates. The dog follows her into the house.

Later, Victor and Ella have an argument. He accuses her of hating his family. She says she doesn't hate them; she likes them. She especially likes them somewhere else. This is an argument they are revisiting; they can have it without thinking too hard. It ends the same way: Ella says she's sorry, she does like his family; she's tired is all. Victor laces their fingers together and believes her.

―――――――――

Ella and Rolan are painting the hallway red. Actually, Rolan is painting and Ella is watching. She notices the rip in his jeans, the way they sag a little in the back; it's an appealing sag, one you could close with your hand. She is thinking of what she will not do. She will not touch his back; his sharp shoulder blades. She will not touch that tooth in the front of his mouth, the crooked one. She won't offer the swimming pool again because she might sound ridiculous. The phone rings.

She answers it only because the machine is nearly full; there are already too many messages stacked up — Victor's mother, his children, his ex-wife. Ella doesn't listen to them because of the tone she hears, especially from his mother. The plaintive, somewhat martyred voice, announcing the time of her call, containing an accusation: *where are you?*

She picks it up in the kitchen. It's Victor's mother.

"Oh dear," she says to Ella, rapidly. "Tell Victor his grandmother's back in the hospital. She's picked something up somewhere. They think it's turned into pneumonia."

"Pneumonia?" says Ella, half-listening. The dog is barking. Someone has pulled into the driveway.

"At her age, pneumonia's a very bad thing. They've asked the family to come down."

"How awful. I'm so sorry. I'll try to reach him."

She walks back to the hallway. Rolan is painting, meticulously, carefully. She considers his girlish waist. He reminds her of Victor's daughters, the clear skin and slender frame, his capacity for delight, at the dog, at his own painstaking work.

She taught the girls to dive just this week, calling to them to keep their legs together, point their toes. There was a moment after the dive when they were still underwater; Ella was poised on the edge, breathing air, aware of her lungs, the contractions of her chest. What did they think, swimming back to the surface? Opening their eyes to the rise of the pool's bottom, touching it, perhaps, with their hands, drifting up, breaking out to the sound of her voice.

How was it, they shouted, heads bobbing, faces expectant.

Great. Perfect. Terrible. Your legs went to hell.

"There's a place right there," she says to Rolan now, a little sharply, "Where it's streaking." She walks away before she sees his face, where she imagines is surprise and defeat.

She goes upstairs and takes a shower. She dries her hair, standing in front of the mirror, wrapped in Victor's robe. She puts on conservative clothes, khakis, a white shirt. She pulls her hair back in a way she knows Victor hates. He likes her messed, sexy, kittenish. He wants everything from her, a mother, a centerfold, a chef. (She knows he would say, no, I love everything about her; I love the way the air smells when she exhales.)

The day is falling again. There's a crescent moon visible in the sky, like a cut fingernail. A shard of moon. She drives slowly, more carefully than she usually does. When the dog sleeps, they call him a dog-shrimp because of the way he curls his front legs, like you could hang him on the edge of a cocktail glass. He can shrink himself like this, but it seems to double his weight.

The hospital is a good distance, but traffic isn't bad. She parks in the small lot near the entrance. The last time she was here she stepped into snow, chilling her ankles, but now it's just the afternoon that meets her legs, a wide band of sunlight across her shoes. There are two entrances, and for no good reason she takes the one she doesn't like, through the nursing home. The woman at the desk wears a hair net, calls her honey. Honey, she says, go on in. Ella does.

Through dim, greenish hallways, she steps around old people in their wheelchairs, apologizing under her breath, looking away. If the place were an ocean, these figures would be like the survivors of shipwrecks, waiting for rescue, for hypothermia, for the pleasure of drowning. She takes the patient elevator and rides up with an old man on a stretcher and an orderly; the man's face is slack and lifeless, the kind of face that might suddenly sit up and yell boo, scare the daylights out of you.

———

Victor, too, gets a message from his mother but puts it aside. He has meetings, an appointment to get his hair cut. He will go home early and surprise Ella. He has dual motives; he hopes that his arrival will please her, but he half-hopes he will catch her at something. What, he isn't sure, but there's a distinct tingle he feels, turning down the street, steering his car into the driveway, hearing the crunch of gravel under the tires. There's the boy working at the house, for one thing. As he leaves the office, he passes his boss's secretary; she makes a crack about facial reconstruction, skin grafts. Victor smiles tightly; the dog bite again. He feels bad enough, and it's Ella's fault anyway, the dog's unpredictable behavior. It's because she coddles him, spoons with him in their bed, feeds him too much protein. He makes up his mind to put him on a diet, be more firm.

Last week, after his family left, before the argument, Ella had asked him what his grandmother had said when she spoke in Yiddish. Victor shook his head, said he had no idea. He did though; the language is still there; he can make out enough to get the drift. She was complaining about the way his two older daughters were sitting, with their legs drawn up and their knees wide. Unladylike, inappropriate — he had caught that much. They're too old for that, she was saying.

He thinks, maybe; if your frame of reference for adulthood is childbirth at fourteen and three-quarters, maybe that's true. But his girls aren't yet eleven; they're babies. That's what his mother had replied, at the time. There's time, she had told his grandmother, enough time for that. Why didn't he tell this to Ella? She would have found it funny, quaint. Then she would have snorted, said something typically Ella, something patronizing. The kind of remark Liz would never make.

Victor has a small crush on Liz. He likes her fine features, her gentle manner, her unfailing kindness. He thinks about Liz abstractly — not her breasts or her legs or even her parted mouth; he thinks instead of her neat loafers, her smell of soap, the look of her hair in the sun. Where Ella is tough and moody, Liz is serene, sweet. Both women are mannered, a little stuck on protocol, but where in Ella this can manifest as sneering, slightly superior, in Liz it is quiet and gracious. The way she was with his family, for instance, how she bent and kissed his grandmother's cheek, managed to be interested and delighted all afternoon. And there was Ella, in the background, vanishing for long spaces, needing to be retrieved from the kitchen, or once from in front of the television, where he found her watching a political talk show. As he drives, he cuts the two women up and pastes them back together in a way he finds more pleasing.

Alone in the house, Rolan puts down his paint roller and plays with the dog. He stands next to the swimming pool and throws a stick down the long length of lawn. He takes his shirt off and lies down in the dry grass, feels it prick the skin of his back. The dog lies down next to him, falls asleep. Rolan too feels heavy and tired; his arms are flecked red. He lies with one hand across his face, shading his eyes. Somewhere nearby there is music. All these people are unspeakably rich; Rolan lives in a cheap apartment above a store that sells live poultry. The stench is sickening. What he told Ella is not true; he has no memories of swimming in any river. He grew up in Los Angeles in an apartment that smelled of cooking grease, brothers who played with guns and knives, a father who was quick with his belt, with a closed fist. His recollections of water are public swimming pools tinged green, with slimy walls and suspicious pockets of warmth.

When Ella is there, he calls her Miss Ella; when he sits at night with his friends, drinking cheap beer and telling lies, he calls her the rich lady I fuck in the swimming pool. He has a growing number of filthy stories he tells about Ella; in them she is voracious and wildly experienced, pleading and insatiable. His friends listen with sly smiles, wiping their thin mustaches, asking for a crack at Ella. He has made her a lusty cartoon, a woman drawn in bold lines in a lurid comic book, breasts popping, a waist you could close with your fingers. The things she says appear in fat bubbles, coming from big, red lips: Do it harder, do it again, don't stop. In some of these stories, he includes the dog. This lady is a freak, he tells his friends; she is crazy for fucking anything.

When Rolan wakes, he swims. He shucks off his stiff jeans and slides into the cool blue water. Another thing Ella doesn't know is that her invitation came too late; he has been swimming all along, every time she leaves the house. He is not worried about being caught at this; he believes that Ella's invitation is sincere. Also, he has begun to believe his own stories and has an elaborate fantasy of Ella coming home and finding him in the pool, dropping her clothes at the edge, swimming toward him. Now the dog swims with him; they swim lazy laps side by side. When Rolan watches him underwater, the dog looks like one of Santa's reindeer, legs moving in a parody of flight, slow, languid, suspended.

When he's dried himself off with his shirt, he returns to the house, climbs the stairs to the bedrooms on the second floor. Ella and Victor have his and hers bathrooms. Hers is a poppy red that Rolan painted weeks ago; his is wood-paneled, masculine. He slides open Ella's drawers and fingers her makeup, puts his face to her underwear, lies down on the bed. Her jewelry box is enameled, a series of tiny drawers, a bureau on a small scale. He fingers earrings and rings but replaces them. At home he has a shoebox full of panties that he shows to his friends. He describes the manner in which he drew them from Ella's pale hips, what followed.

Celia is fastened to machines: one tube feeds oxygen into her nose, one drips fluid into her arm; others have less obvious motives. Her breathing is labored. She feels as if she's inside a tunnel, listening to herself gasp. The sound is magnified; it blots out everything else. It offers the room and space for new corridors of thought, of memory. She follows them, opens the doors they present, passes through, finds others, opens them as well. She does not struggle to keep a memory straight or true. Her thoughts are not wandering off, as she is used to; instead she is swimming through them cleanly. There are no annoying obstructions, tangents.

Her husband, her cousin, was kind but determined. He had not married a squeamish girl; he had chosen her for her familiarity with hard work, her bossy, efficient manner with farm animals and children. That she was infatuated with him he saw as a passing aggravation, one he could weather.

Her mother had come the day of the birth; it was true. Celia was just nearing her fifteenth birthday, but she was not afraid of what was going to happen to her; she wanted to get on with it. Had he been reading the paper? That part was likely true as well. He read news of local interest and the prices of things. The pot roast had gone into the oven in the morning. If Victor knew anything, he would know that you can't birth a baby in the afternoon and get a roast on the table by suppertime, not without planning and forethought.

In pictures she can still see herself as she was then. In one she is standing with her new family, in a smudged print dress, near the edge of the photograph. One foot is trapped on the photographer's drape; she was afraid to move it for fear of dragging the thing down. In the picture she looks uncomfortable and heavy, a potato of a girl, with a thrusting chin, fists closed at her side. There are two babies here as well, serious babies in identical white gowns. When she remembers this picture, she sees an empty space, the spot where the other baby would have been.

That space in front of her, where she seems to stand alone, she left for her dead baby, the pot-roast baby. That baby would have been three at the age the picture was taken, old enough for short pants and to stand in front of her, grabbing at her skirt.

All that for nothing. All the grunting and pain and blood for that tiny, breathless fist of a child. She was like a cow in the field that day, like many she'd seen firsthand, getting up and walking away from a still calf, shaking loose of the gore. She turned her face as her mother wrapped the failure in a bedsheet, disappeared down the staircase.

In the kitchen below, her mother would have told the news to her nephew, Celia's husband. Celia herself has no idea what words were spoken or what he might have said, or thought. She knows, though, that in the morning the pot roast was gone. The pan sat on the stove; what was left of the hacked-at lump of meat lay in congealing juices, surrounded by softened carrots, gold-edged parsnips. Left dishes, a fork and knife crosswise, a napkin on the seat of chair, and the chair not even pushed back to the table but stranded in the middle of the kitchen.

Someone is speaking to her, pulling her away, up to the surface. The voice is unfamiliar; no, now it's that girl, Victor's shiksa. Celia opens her eyes, or she believes that she does. There is someone there, and yes, it is shaped like that girl, the skinny one. Celia suspects her of encouraging Victor to lose weight; he looks drawn and thin since he has been seeing her. What is she doing here? I must be dying, Celia thinks; this is not a girl who visits hospitals out of kindness, or even obligation. Obviously, I must be dying.

"I wanted to talk to you," Ella says now. She sits on the corner of the bed; her weight makes the bed shift, the tubes adjust. She looks at them carefully, afraid something might have been dislodged.

"You too," says Celia, and the words come out strung together, misshapen. "A recipe," she says, "I wanted to give you a recipe." She isn't sure why she's said this, only that it seems important.

"What?" says Ella. "I don't understand. I wanted to talk about Victor."

"He was very fat," says Celia. "He was a fat, healthy baby." Ella laughs, and Celia sees that she doesn't understand.

Now something else occurs to her; she says, "My children are at my apartment, putting names on my things."

"What?" says Ella again. She is staring around the room now, anxiously. Shouldn't there be a doctor around? She is thinking, this woman looks too sick to be alone for long.

Celia is remembering when she returned from the hospital the last time, after the hip operation. She came home to find little sticky things, notes, stuck on the undersides of her furniture. She had found them by falling once — the sudden view she had of the bottom of her coffee table. They were on nearly everything. Each note had the name of one of her six living children; on some the first name had been crossed out and replaced by another, as if there had been an argument, bargaining. Later she had rearranged the notes, dragged herself around and put them back randomly. Two notes she removed entirely and replaced with new ones. These had the name of the pot-roast baby, Leonard. She gave him the Russian tea samovar and the little marble table in the hallway. Let them wonder, she thought.

If she had the breath to say all this, she would tell it to Ella. Celia thinks she would appreciate this kind of humor, this sort of retributive prank. A skinny person's joke, a little sly, a little nasty.

Ella shifts on the bed, rises, and pats the blankets around Celia's shoulders. The questions she was going to ask now seem foolish, and none were about Victor anyway. She had thought to ask Celia about when she was a woman, not just Victor's grandmother: about dresses she had had, places she had not visited, about dreams no one imagined she might be entitled to. Ella had wanted to offer to dress her hair for her, in any way she liked, and to hear whatever stories Celia wanted to tell — not just those that Victor wants to gather, to shelve and recollect at his convenience.

Victor is deadheading hydrangeas in the garden. He isn't answering the telephone. He misses two calls from his mother saying that they are on the way to the hospital, he should come, and one from Ella saying she is on her way back. He misses a call from Liz as well, saying that she has finally been to the doctor, had her glands felt up, prescribed antibiotics.

Earlier, in the bedroom when he changed his clothes, he had smelled something he didn't like. Not Ella's scent, not his. He followed it from Ella's pillow to her bathroom; he lifted his nose to the air the way the dog does. He felt angry and confused. He took the clippers from their case and headed out toward the hydrangea. Now he is snipping dying flowers and dead ones. He smokes and drops the ends in the mulch.

When he hears Ella pull into the driveway, he stops what he's doing. He is standing near the pool when he sees something he doesn't recognize lying across a lounge chair. It's a man's T-shirt but boy-sized, speckled with red paint. What the fuck, he thinks. He bunches it up and stuffs it in the waistband of his jeans. He is smoking there when she comes out; her hair is pulled back tightly; she looks sharp.

"There you are," she says. "Shit. Where were you?"

"Where were you?" Victor has his hand on the bunch of cloth at his back. The smell is the one he found in the bedroom. He pulls the shirt from his pants, waves it at her, as if flagging her down. "What's this? What is it?"

At a cocktail party, Liz listens to her husband tell another conceit. Asked where he is from, she hears him say he grew up in London. He spent six months there as an exchange student. She thinks of Victor — funny and honest and true.

From his car, Victor calls Rolan and fires him over the answering machine. When the phone rings a few moments later, he pulls to the side of the road. While traffic flashes by, his mother tells him it's too late. He considers turning around but then goes ahead to the hospital. At home, Ella will be loving the dog. His beautiful children will be having baths in his old house, the one he still pays for. The youngest girl is the prettiest. He thinks about the other two, the rivalries to come. He thinks about Ella and why she couldn't have been the woman he thought. He puts Liz in the passenger seat next to him, her small hand on his knee. Comforting and assured.

Ella sits down with the dog and watches television. The dog is snoring a little; he has his head on her lap. Hours pass; she drifts off. The car that pulls into her dream is one she thinks she recognizes; this must be why the dog barely shifts, only yawns a little. They pile out in the driveway; young boys with shaved heads and muscle shirts, all ripple and swagger. Speaking Spanish, excited and drunk. They gather in knots outside the window and then spread out, heading toward the many doors. It's a vulnerability of the house, the dozens of ways to get in. There are four doors off the porch alone. She lifts the dog's head, heavy as lead, and gets up. If she is awake, her legs will be numb from the weight of him; if she is dreaming, she will move like the wind, like a panicked swimmer toward shore, until she wakes with a jolt and a racing heart.

Celia opens another door, one that is less solid, a shimmering, watery door. Inside it, her husband embraces her and finally says he misses the pot-roast baby. He is sorry for never mentioning it, never saying a word of comfort. But now here, inside this door, from behind, comes Leonard, tall and strong and handsome. He comes up on her cousin-husband from the back and puts his big arms around his shoulders. He gives his father a strong, youthful shake, full of affection and camaraderie. She sees they know each other. Leonard winks at his mother and smiles. He holds out his hands and draws her in. She disappears inside him, and it's just like everything before, but reversed.

Once

The postcard that arrives in Lydia's mailbox one late summer afternoon surprises her. It is a photograph of a painting, though it takes her a moment to recognize it. First, there is just the impression of whiteness, of a place sun-beaten and washed away. Then houses emerge: barely colored edges appear; they rise vertically from the glossy paper and take on a shape, an impression, of something familiar. She turns the card in her hand and studies it. The postcard advertises an old lover's paintings, an upcoming show at a gallery. Through the pale houses, she detects the faint change of light that signals water. Malcolm has painted it as though standing right in the middle of those narrow streets, the houses thrown up around the painter, erected in pale, watery strokes. The painting, she sees by reading the back of the card, is called *Proposal*.

Lydia processes all this, standing on the quiet road near the mailbox. It is a bright spring day; the hostas are like garlands at the feet of two tall hemlocks that flank the drive. She looks at them — their fleshy leaves, milky centers — with the sense that the day has been somehow altered. She had not thought of this man, or those distant events, in years, but as she does, there is a twinge she can't quite label, or properly name.

Examining the postcard, Lydia thinks it was certainly the town's pallidity — the pale, boxy houses in pastel shades — that is most resonant, that might account for everything. In her memory, the entire seaside town seemed the victim of glare, everything cast in watery, colorless light. The streets were cobbled, she recalls that, and the ocean — with France visible, a lump in the far distance — seemed the same flinty shade as the houses, the sky, even the rental car that had brought them there. The town's name was Deal.

——— ———

Malcolm and Lydia were in England, combining an antique-buying trip with a few days in the country. They had stayed with Malcolm's friends — a fellow antique dealer who walked around in a haze of hashish, his horsey, horse-faced wife, their wide-eyed son. The boy's name was Colin, she remembers quite suddenly. Caroline and Derek were his parents.

The three lived in an enormous stone house crammed with their finds. They favored heavy Gothic furniture and frayed, patched kilims layered over one another so that the footing was always tricky; you might drop several inches walking across a seemingly stable surface. There was low, sporadic lighting, and dust bunnies skidded across wide, rough floors. An old Aga stove squatted in a corner of the kitchen; the pantry was filled with Bovril and Nutella. A glance inside showed shelves thick with crumbs and mouse droppings, pieces of horse tack — mossy snaffle bits and pelhams — side by side with cereal and biscuits.

When they arrived, Lydia found Caroline immediately unfriendly. Derek wafted around in his own smog, tall and stooped and nondescript. He fastened them occasionally with a wondering half-smile or burst into peals of inappropriate laughter. It was clear to Lydia quickly that they — she and Malcolm — were not especially welcome, not even expected. Malcolm had called from the car rental agency at Heathrow and announced their arrival. Lydia sensed, rather than heard, the reluctance of the invitation. She was amazed Malcolm had not arranged this beforehand.

She remembers he had turned to her and shrugged it off, saying, "They're always in the middle of a ruckus."

"Maybe it's not a good time," she said. "Maybe we should get a hotel."

He said, "It's never a good time with them. It's fine. Don't worry."

They arrived in the dark, lurching up a rutted path that no sane person would think led anywhere. The house emerged like a monster, looming up in stone angles; light exited randomly from a few leaded windows. At the gate that barred the entrance — a sagging wooden affair that wouldn't have deterred an ambitious sheep — a pack of shaggy dogs met them, howling and snarling. Malcolm got out of the car and hipped the gate wide. He was lost for a moment in the headlights, the jostling dog bodies.

In the blackness, as they drove up the pocked lane, flanked by dogs, a woman on horseback cantered into view. The headlights showed her jumping a coop into the drive. She pulley-reined the horse up next to the car and leaned down. Malcolm lowered the window.

She said, "I'm having a problem with the bloody side mirror on the Jeep. I can't get the parts, can I? Will you send them? Hello," she said without enthusiasm, waving in at Lydia. In the dark she was just a hunched figure on a massive horse, wild-haired, in a great woolly sweater. The animal blew the scent of oats and sweat into the mini. The windows fogged. The woman straightened up again and slapped the horse's neck. "But really, Mal, I'm screwed. I need them sent from America. I'll just put this stupid horse up and then I'll be in. Derek's somewhere, as usual."

Inside the house, when Caroline finally appeared, a marital argument was clearly in progress. It had been interrupted, but they found their places quickly enough. Formal introductions were brief, terse, altogether dismissive. Caroline and Derek, Lydia noticed, spoke to one another in sidelong barbs, if at all. They all stood in the harsh light of the kitchen — suitcases still in the rental car — and stared at one another. Then Caroline began to busy herself with mysterious tasks. She flung herself into motion, hands flapping, drying, uncorking. She wore a horse's martingale strung around her neck, and she swiped at it with a dishcloth, making punishing motions along its length. Lydia thought she had the kind of fingers that could rend leather. A little boy appeared in the doorway then. He came in and lingered at their feet, staring, touching the edges of things — legs of tables, Lydia's boots, doorknobs of cupboards — until Caroline slapped at him, and he scuttled a short distance away and touched other things.

"We weren't expecting you." Her voice was not especially light, not really joking.

Lydia watched Malcolm. He did not respond. He moved around the kitchen as if he belonged; he leaned against the Aga and began to talk about something. She noticed his earnest persistence, his oblivion to his audience; he talked of his business in America, of what he was hunting for, how long he'd be.

All the while, Derek and Caroline moved around them. Lydia was standing backed up to a cupboard, pulling at the neck of her sweater. Derek made small doglike circles near the Aga, as if he might at any moment throw himself down against its warmth and nap. Caroline seemed frantic in comparison, not hospitably but belligerently going about her business. She extracted a knife from the sink — not a terribly clean one — sliced a slab of bread and handed it to the child, who took it without comment or expression. He was maybe eight, this Colin, with nearly white hair cut jaggedly, perhaps by the same serrated knife she was holding.

When he came back from the pantry, the bread covered thickly with some brown substance, he dragged a stool to the counter and climbed onto it. He pulled an old biscuit tin closer and opened it, withdrawing fistfuls of words and letters cut from books and magazines — curling strips of glossy magazine paper, smudged newsprint, the thick, yellowy paper that children's books were once printed on. He began to arrange them, pushing them around the wooden surface of the island. Lydia rose up onto her toes to watch. She watched him fashion sentences like *Sam hurts the purple butterfly,* and *Mummy eats dog eyeballs.* Lydia raised her eyebrows. No one else noticed. Caroline glanced over, not at the sentences themselves, but her eyes rested briefly on the biscuit tin.

She said, "There's not a single book left in this house with all the words in. Is there Colin?"

Colin made no sign he'd heard. He made: *Dead rotting kittens ooze shit bugger cunt.*

Beyond the overlit kitchen was the dark remainder of the house. It seemed to stretch for miles; it might contain endless unknown animals and humans, chained or otherwise captive. Lydia shivered a little and Caroline noticed; her eyes flickered. After an instant, she turned back to the sink and began mixing something in a large plastic bucket.

She said to Malcolm, "You can have your usual room. I don't have any idea if there are sheets in there. You might try the laundry, but I've really no idea." She shrugged.

Derek said, "Bitch," but as he was face to face with the Aga, crouching down, there was no way to tell whom he was addressing.

Later, Malcolm took Lydia's hand and led her into the hallway. She tripped over riding boots and a collection of canvases, stacked and leaning against a commode chair. She said, "Christ."

Malcolm laughed; he had laughed when he was uncomfortable or when there was nothing else to say. Down the hall, around several sharp turns, he pushed open the door to a small room, no less cluttered. There was a single bed, an overpowering smell of dust and closeness; the room screamed for air. Lydia looked around for a window she might open. From a pile on the floor, Malcolm found a blanket, a thin stained pillow, a torn floral sheet. Lydia sniffed them.

"Tomorrow," she said firmly. "A hotel."

"I should tell you," Malcolm said to her as he took off his clothes, "I slept with her once."

Lydia stood fully dressed and lowered herself onto the sagging mattress. She took her coat and laid it over her, then removed her sweater and balled it under her head for a pillow.

"Why should you tell me that?" Lydia folded her arms behind her head.

"In case you sensed anything. It was a huge mistake."

"Great news." Lydia slunk lower in the bed, thinking of hotels and starched sheets and breakfasts delivered on trays.

Malcolm put his hand on her bra, leaned up on one elbow, and looked down at her. "Hey," he said. "Would this be in poor taste?"

"The worst," she said and turned her head away.

She left his hand lying uselessly on her satin-covered breast. She dreamed fitfully, of Malcolm and Caroline entwined in a horse's stall, amid straw and manure, surrounded by hooves and fetlocks. The eyes of that boy watched from somewhere above. Cartoon bubbles from his mouth spat words like *fuck* and *whore* and *Mummy*. They arranged themselves into descriptive sentences while Caroline looked up and said encouragingly, "That's a good one, Colin. Try another."

A few days later they'd driven to the sea. It was pleasant enough, the green countryside skidding by, cows and sheep ambling across roads, the chancy roundabouts that Malcolm took too carelessly, his cheap sunglasses — he thought gaudiness was funny — hiding his eyes from her. The drive had that odd quality of suspended time, the unfamiliar roads and road signs, the landscape glistening wet and the off-putting sense of driving on the wrong side of the road. That sense of wrongness never quite left her, so she put herself into a mild state of trance to avoid thinking about it.

While they drove, Malcolm talked, and she tallied what he'd had to drink that day. Her best estimate was three pints of Guinness and however much he'd swallowed of the flask of scotch he held between his legs. When Malcolm drank, he talked endlessly and incomprehensibly about art. Braque, he might say, in disgust. Or, Art — What do art critics know about art? Lydia tuned him out. Back home, Malcolm's paintings covered the walls of the dairy barn he lived in, also the upstairs of his antique shop. Lydia found them unsettling and possibly not very good; she hoped they were over her head.

During the drive she had also been thinking how odd to be in love — if that was not overstating matters — with a man who admitted to never having read a book. England was their second trip together. On the first — an island vacation to which Lydia had humped an entire separate suitcase of books — Malcolm had simply brought himself, a few pairs of shorts, a collection of ugly sunglasses, and flippers. While she sat on the sand and turned pages, he had stared at the water, hands folded around a glass of rum, and hummed.

Lydia watched the road, gripping the sides of her seat. Over the past several days, they had prowled Derek's low tumbling-down warehouses, traveling in a cloud of his perfumed smoke. The hotel had never materialized. While Lydia followed them, watching her shoes, dodging puddles and strips of rubber and planks with rusty nails thrust upward, Malcolm looked around, appraising, dating, stepping over and under debris, identifying pieces he might be interested in. They ducked under beams, battled cobwebs woven thick as tweed, and peered into murky corners at the shadowy lines and angles of strangers' refuse.

That morning they had visited Derek's last warehouse. There had been a steady, boring downpour. As they pulled away, the sun was a pale, hazy orb behind the grimy smokestack of a factory. The car had paralleled a dank canal, which snaked under bridges and lapped at the edges of towns. Its banks were littered with trash. They passed a group of small boys walking along the waterway, knee-deep in debris and mud. Though the windows were closed, Lydia could tell they were swearing at one another, could imagine the suck of their shoes as they shoved and roughhoused; they were coarse, dirty boys in knee britches, boys she wouldn't want to run into alone. They made her think of Colin, these boys, though they were years older. Despite their youth, they seemed capable of injuring adults, adept at the kind of joyous, colorful taunting at which small boys excel. She turned away, watched the rain spatter the windshield. She'd had a run-in with Colin days earlier; her mind kept returning to it.

She'd been lying in bed, waiting for Malcolm to come out of the shower. She had drifted off, and when the door creaked, she turned to find Colin's sharp little face at the level of the doorknob.

"Hello," she'd said. She pulled the sheet tighter. "Good morning."

"Where's my dad?" he said, looking around the room, into the corners. He had a suspicious face, a canniness he couldn't have yet earned.

"Well, he's not here. I'm certain of that." Lydia sat up and reached for a lamp on the nightstand.

"Is he in the shower then?"

"Malcolm is. I don't know where your dad is. Did you ask your mother?"

The door opened wider and Colin stepped inside. He took an exaggerated stride over the threshold and arrived with a thump near the bottom of the bed.

"I asked her."

For a moment he stared at her rudely; then his eyes roamed the room and landed on a pile of books near Lydia's suitcase.

Lydia, watching him, said, "You like books? I saw all the words you play with. Do you like to read?"

Colin didn't look at her; he moved toward the books and gently kicked the top one off the stack. He said, "I don't play and I don't read. Are there any good words in these?"

Lydia folded her arms across her chest. "What sort?"

"Good ones." His voice held a leisurely impatience.

"Like what?" said Lydia, in the same tone.

Colin looked up and smiled a foxy little smile. "Fuck words. Shit words. Guts. Pus. Rotting stuff. Dead stuff. Animals."

"Are those the kind you like?"

"Those are the kind I work with," he said.

Lydia snorted. "You mean, your medium? Like an artist?"

He looked at her coldly. The toe of his shoe flipped a book cover open and then closed again. Once, twice, three times. Lydia felt ridiculous but still, somehow, competently threatened.

He said, "I bet there are good words in there. I bet I could find them. Tell Dad I was here." Then he turned and left the room without closing the door behind him.

It was an episode she hadn't shared with Malcolm, for no real reason.

Driving to the coast, Lydia shook these thoughts off and said idly, "Have you found anything you like in Derek's crap?"

"That crap is my livelihood," Malcolm said. "That crap pays my bills."

Crap, the word, sounded strange in his accent — heavy on the *p* sound. He turned to grin at her; the plastic sunglasses had swirling purple designs on the sides.

"You'd be surprised, really, at how it cleans up. Derek gets that tat from all over — people's yards and barns and corncribs. You'd be amazed what some people do with their antiques — toss them out in the snow, chop them up for firewood."

"I'm sure I would be. Surprised. Amazed. Flabbergasted."

"You'll see," he said. He smiled, taking no offense. He reached over and grabbed her thigh, squeezed it with pleasure. "That little footstool? Did you notice that?"

"No. What footstool?"

"At Derek's place a few days ago? That piece under the tarp — well, I put it under the tarp. I'm certain it's sixteenth century. The lines? The overpainting. It's that primitive, that rough. Derek wouldn't notice if it bit him."

"Derek wouldn't notice a train bearing down on him. Are you going to buy it?"

He grinned at her. "Sure. But I won't tell him what I'm buying."

"Dodgy," Lydia said and smiled back at him. She pulled her hair up and fastened it behind her head with a clip; she found a spot for the base of her neck on the headrest.

As they drove, she looked at him from the corner of her eye. She admired his surprising good looks, the heavy dark hair he tossed from his eyes, the one crooked incisor that made his smile rakish. Her doubts were still toys she was playing with, rearranging like Colin's endless, curling scraps of paper.

When they arrived in Deal, the streets were shiny and slick from a recent rain. The road wound round the town, and Malcolm parked by the water. There was a fingernail's curve of stony sand, a clutch of ragged birds squawking and hopping, pecking hopefully. Malcolm led her through the streets; the town was strangely silent, as if the rain had washed away not only its color but its residents as well. No sidewalks, she noticed. No people. Emptiness. All the houses faced in on each other; windows stared at windows across narrow ribbons of cobblestone. From the road you saw only the blank backs of houses, as if the town was walled-

off somehow, self-protecting. It was only inside the streets —
which seemed close, overly intimate — that the town's face appeared. There was no central avenue, no street of shops, just a grid
of pale square buildings laid out like a tic-tac-toe game. There
might have been a lace curtain in a window, or a tub of geraniums
at someone's door, but nothing mitigated the impression of pure
wateriness. Even then it felt like a town created by the point of a
paintbrush moving rapidly across stretched canvas. Lydia half-
felt that if she pushed hard enough against a wall or a door, the
whole town might collapse like cardboard — in a great sighing
and rushing of paper, the sound a house of cards makes when you
sweep your hand through its foundation.

Malcolm said, "Do you notice it? How strange this town is?"

Lydia said, "Bleached. Leached. Blanched." The words fell
out like paper thoughts—typeset, clipped from pages. It was as
though they were rustling through her fingers, waiting for verbs.
The town had made her feel suddenly bone-colored and hopeless.

They wandered through the streets and wound up back at the
car; it had taken maybe ten minutes. They had seen just two people: a tan-colored man in a matching raincoat, riding a rusted bi-
cycle — the noise of it creaking over the stones had made her
jump — and a woman's back as she bent over the doorway of her
own house, straightening a rush mat.

Lydia balanced on a concrete parking barrier. This made her
slightly taller than Malcolm. She surveyed the beach for skipping
stones but saw none. The water seemed endlessly shallow; it met
the sky with no perceptible change of hue. She thought she might
walk to France, get a decent meal. A breeze lifted her hair and the
collar of Malcolm's leather jacket, which she smelled as he stepped
closer and put his arms around her. Standing there, smelling hide
and brine and Caroline's soap in his hair, she had the urge to sigh,
to go limp across his shoulders and let herself be carried. Instead
she patted his hair affectionately and warmed her hands briskly
on his back.

"Cold?" he asked.

"Slightly."

"Let's have a nip then, shall we?" Lydia could never tell whether
Malcolm's Britishisms were a habit he fell into in that country or

an affectation for his own amusement. He had lived in America nearly twenty years.

They stepped back into the washed-out streets; he led the way to the pub.

"Want to hear something funny?" Malcolm grabbed her hand; she was holding her cigarettes, and she heard the pack crunch in on itself. "Caroline called me once, totally pissed, and told me Colin was mine."

"Pissed drunk or pissed mad?" Lydia was conscious of not breaking stride at all, not hesitating a beat.

"Both. That's Caroline, right?"

Lydia shrugged. How would she know?

"Silly cow," said Malcolm. "That would be something, wouldn't it?"

They ducked under the pub's low wooden sign and stepped into the room, into smoke and conversation, equally thick. Heads turned. Faces swiveled toward them and then away, but not before looking them up and down, with no particular expression. A young woman stood behind the bar, polishing glasses, smoking urgently. She had canted hips, the lifted chin and exposed throat of a brassy, brawling girl. Her eyes seemed to view them from a height; there was not a flicker of warmth in them. The room returned to its conversation. It seemed to be one large discussion, involving people seated at tables and at the bar; it covered football and money troubles and fag borrowing. Lydia felt edgy with unease and something more; her skin prickled.

They sat across a small table from one another and could not think of anything to say. They pushed their glasses around; Lydia smoked one cigarette after another. They held each other's hands and stared down at them as though looking for something.

"Listen," Malcolm said finally. "I know we haven't known each other all that long."

But Lydia cut him off. She said, "Don't."

This surprised her actually, that she'd said that. She glanced around the edge of the dirty red curtain into the glistening, uneven streets. She was thinking of the state she'd found her books in the night before, the neat rectangles made by scissors, the way words had been cleverly split and excised. He had found syllables he'd wanted and small runs of letters that could be easily pieced together with others. She hadn't imagined all the possibilities that words contained, but he'd made them obvious.

A roar of laughter went up around the pub, and Lydia, staring out at the wet, worn cobblestones, thought momentarily of this town she found herself in, of the dull gleam of the water, the bleached fishing boats and seines, the graying stones and tattered seabirds.

Soon after that, Lydia had gone to Spain. She'd had a business meeting; Malcolm was to arrange for his shipment and fly home alone.

She called Malcolm from Spain, but they had little to say to each other. He'd gone north to Hull to visit his mother, and she heard him whispering on the landing about the dole, the public housing, how he'd walked the whole city looking for a hotel she'd be willing to stay in. "When you come to meet Mum," he'd said. And then, "This fucking river, it's like gravy."

"Can't wait," she'd said, standing in her hotel room. Spain was gold and blue — the hotel itself was pink, really pink — the land alternately lush and arid, humming with music, with insects, with the vibrant movement of young hips, the flash of a matador's beaded vest.

She had met her husband, in fact, on that trip to Spain, and when she'd returned home, she'd seen Malcolm only twice more. Now, with so many years gone by, with grown children and a fine settled life, Lydia is unsure of the details. They have the same unstable edges as the buildings Malcolm painted, blurriness of overpainting, the slippery feel of revisionism.

The proper end of their romance is lost in a shuffle of facts and inconsequences — an argument, a thrown pack of cigarettes, too many martinis. All that remain are deceptive fragments, the triangular shards of scenes. It hardly matters.

Lydia does remember one of the few things Caroline did say to her, one dark afternoon in the kitchen, while Malcolm was off wandering somewhere with Derek and they found themselves together accidentally. That afternoon she recalls with surprising clarity. There was the clamor of the Aga, the smell of Bovril, a film of biscuit crumbs across the island. She remembers the two cabinet doors that hung open, a sweet wrapper near her left boot, the edge of a windcheater that hung on a rack beyond the kitchen door, the strange quality of its hanging, empty sleeve.

Caroline had stood with her back at the sink, holding a mug of tea between her hands. Lydia was trying to make conversation.

"It won't work, you know," Caroline said, breaking into Lydia's sentence — something about dinner. "You and Mal. It's ridiculous."

Lydia didn't feel surprised particularly, nor bristly — rather curious. Caroline had such a formidable certainty about her, the kind often found in women who are sure around horses. Since the first night, Lydia had wondered about Malcolm's wording, describing his intimacy with Caroline. He had said, "once." Had he meant one event, or did the word imply a longer span of couplings, as in "once upon a time"?

"Why's that?" Lydia asked her.

Caroline snickered. "First place, you're so fucking superior. Don't you think he'll get sick of that, sooner or later?"

Lydia started.

"That's right," Caroline said. "You're not fooling me. You think you're better than him and won't let him forget it. Your clothes, your hotels, your snotty book talk; you're a pain. *Lydia*." Her voice was hateful but still, somehow, completely free of jealousy.

But Lydia said anyway, "I know about the two of you. I'm not surprised you're saying that."

"The two of who?" said Caroline. "Please. We had it off a few times," she waved it away with a hand. "What, did he tell you about Colin too?" She slurped her tea and plunked the mug down on the sink. She wore a sly grin.

Lydia stared at her. "What about him?"

The door slammed then and they both jumped. Derek and Mal came in with dripping boots; they sloshed across the kitchen to the stove and pressed their hands against it.

Caroline retrieved her tea. She said, "Derek, who is Colin's father again?"

Derek picked up his head and coughed. Mal looked at Lydia; she shrugged.

Derek didn't turn around, he said, "Postman? Milkman? Bloke down the pub? Possibly me?"

"Possibly," said Caroline. "In all bloody likelihood. More's the pity." She shot Lydia a filthy look. "Anyway," she said. "Lydia wanted to know. Now I'm going to wrap that horse." She slammed out.

"I didn't," said Lydia quickly. "I certainly did not."

Derek looked at her in his cloudy way; he shook his head back and forth. "Don't mind her," he said. "She's a prime cunt, is Caroline."

Colin's head appeared around the door then. What did he do all day? Who looked after him? He surveyed the room with narrow eyes and then backed away, but not before Lydia saw him eye the tin of letters; she could tell he was contemplating a dash across the kitchen, a seize and retreat.

"Excuse me," she said, after a few minutes. She took the biscuit tin and started out of the kitchen. Even then, days later, the house was confusing, dark and twisting. She found Colin in a small room with a fireplace blazing; he was stroking a tabby cat with excessive force.

"I brought you these," she said. She put the tin down on the floor, stood with her back to the fireplace.

"Why?" he said. "I didn't want them."

"Oh," said Lydia. "My mistake. I thought you did."

"My mum hates you," he told her. The cat squeezed from his grip and careened out of the room. "She says you're a stuck-up American bitch."

"You did a number on my books, you know. But I don't plan to tell."

Colin shrugged. "Don't care if you do."

Lydia sighed. "I'll leave these in case you want them later." She walked to the door and then stopped. "Malcolm's not your dad, for your information. Derek is."

Colin made a derisive noise. He used his nose, his mouth, his gnomish little features. "Can't believe you fell for that," he said. "Course he's not." He dumped the biscuit tin over and began rooting around in it.

He made small sounds of pleasure, finding what he wanted. He shoved the paper bits together and apart, rearranging them with little hoots of laughter.

"What do you mean? Hey Colin? Fell for what?"

Colin looked up at her, wide-eyed — suddenly, inexplicably, his age. "They had you *on*, all of them. Well, me too. Malcolm's my *dad*? For chrissakes. That's funny. Who'd believe that?"

On the floor at his feet, before Lydia stalked away, she saw what he'd made: *Stupid American bitch.*

The next day they'd driven to Deal. The next day Malcolm had said those casual — or not so casual — words. It had all dropped apart then, like the lost stitches in Caroline's sweaters, like incoherence spread across a kitchen table, a scatter of smudged words, ugly possibilities.

Now, Lydia studies Mal's blocky, careful penmanship, unchanged over the years. He might have married too, for all she knows. Lydia thinks of her own husband, her successful, reasonable children. Colin, she thinks, likely grew up to take his place among the other skinny, loutish boys who had hung around Derek's warehouses. He would be proficient at catcalls, vulgar jokes, other small cruelties. She remembers his pale little face, his tin of letters, his sly, unkempt mother.

Lydia takes the postcard inside the house and slips it into a kitchen drawer. She doesn't keep it for the reasons her husband will accuse her of, when he discovers it one day among the batteries and photo negatives, the scissors, twine, and Scotch tape. She keeps it instead to remind herself of a less certain woman who once visited a pale fishing village a stone's throw from France — a young woman who could be undone by half-truths and pawned by children.

Telling Stories

Cecily was the Lullaby Lady on afternoon radio; she worked three to six every weekday. The station was on Main Street, just above a chocolate shop with a pink and black awning. You came through a glass door and up a flight of cement stairs into the front room. The place, every inch of it, always smelled of nougat and nuts. Still, it seemed a little glamorous. Cecily's job was to read children's stories over the microphone, and she liked the quiet closed-in-ness of it, the stale air and the intimacy of the booth.

At the time, the station manager's name was Walter; he had a receding hairline that Cecily liked to rib him about. Believe me, she got away with that sort of thing long after it should have been becoming. But back then it was easy for her. She had hair so thick you could lose jewelry in it, flashy eyes that went from green to gold, and a slim little figure she kept her whole life, without even trying.

She got the job using all those things; she had no qualifications to be a Lullaby Lady, someone you would trust impressionable ears to when they came home from school. Still, she learned to pitch her voice low and read slowly, to inflect the right parts of words, to be suspenseful when it was called for. The rest of her life was influenced by that time next to the microphone. She always spoke like she was telling stories, building to a climax. She had a whispering, overdramatic manner. Her one valuable piece of advice to me was, "Enunciate."

At the time she was living with Aunt Prudence in the attic of a Victorian house on Mauve Street. She had come from Canada with her mother after her father had run off with the woman from the opera. Aunt Pru took in Elizabeth and her four daughters, of whom Cecily was one. She even took in that solid rosewood piano, a monstrous instrument that made the floor groan when it was moved into the front room. The girls stayed on there after Elizabeth died, not long after the move. (I've kept the obituary, saying that my grandmother had been "claimed"—like a coat or a hat, like lost luggage.)

They would have missed Canada and the Laurentians, the four of them left in Ohio, missed ice-skating and mountains and the winter life—skiing and dogsledding and shaggy ponies with ice-encrusted manes. When they were together, infrequently, years later, they told stories that made each other howl: pet dogs or children falling through ice, stories of daring rescues and girlish pluckiness; games, pretending to be blind or that they spoke no English; the endless tricks they played on one another. They were like Little Women, I thought when I heard these things, sweet and fearless and irrepressible. And I envied them even though they were old, even though their breasts sagged and their faces were weary.

They were all tolerant, halfhearted mothers, mothers you could distract or wait out; there was always something else to capture their attention, take their minds off you. But they were sticklers for manners, for thank-you notes and apologies. They liked children in white gloves and pigtails, children who read books quietly. They encouraged privacy, self-sufficiency, layered clothing.

When Cecily was living in Ohio, in the attic on Mauve Street, being the Lullaby Lady on the afternoon shift, she fell a little bit in love with Walter of the receding hairline. The feeling was mutual, and before long Walter said he wanted to marry her, but he was, sad to report, otherwise married. Still, Cecily liked the secrecy of it, the Byzantine quality of their meetings, the vinyl smell of his big family car. She was wearing neat little suits then, carrying small purses and wearing hairpieces — all the rage at the time. She plucked her eyebrows very thin, with a big, shocked arch in the center. I imagine they touched each other rather tentatively, sliding together across the wide, ribbed car seat, brushing hands in the control room, throwing sidelong glances over the traffic report. He would have listened to her, I think, when she read stories over the air. Maybe his own children listened as well, driving in that car, going wherever people took children in those days. He might have said to them, "Listen to the Lullaby Lady. Doesn't she have a lovely voice? Doesn't she tell a nice story?"

This may even have been something they giggled about together, smoking cigarettes in that car, drinking from a silver flask. They might have parked in the cemetery, out near the airstrip, where the gravestones stretch in every direction like a spill of teeth. The car would have been damp with that heat, that blood-buzz, that friction of not touching. And when he told her about listening to her on the radio, it would have reminded her of her own father, taking her to the opera in Montreal, pointing out the tall woman in the pearls and the pale dress. The one in the red velvet box with the opera glasses, the one of whom he said, "Tell me, Cecily, isn't that the most beautiful woman you have ever seen?" But perhaps, too, Walter wanted to rattle her; she was so self-assured, so magnificently imperial. And she was barely twenty-three.

They went on like that for some time, Cecily and Walter, and he would have made her certain promises. How else could she have continued, being so well brought up, so mannered? There would have been that to deal with. But he must have had some flash, some sex appeal, and he must have made her laugh. Of course, when she came up pregnant, things changed in a blink.

She was young and unmarried and living in that attic, that out-of-tune piano all that remained of the people she had arrived with. The other sisters were gone by then, to college or to husbands and homes of their own.

A chill would have fallen over the radio station, over Walter and Cecily, over the chocolate shop. The smell must have nauseated her. What could either of them do? He kept a brave face on for a while, Walter did, and when he made her those promises, she began to believe them; what choice did she have? They were going to run off together, drive away at night in that big car and make some life together somewhere else.

I can see her standing on the street in front of the chocolate shop, on the narrow sidewalk, in the dark, the call letters of the radio station etched in smoky script on the door behind her. In a traveling suit and sensible shoes, a cloth suitcase, her hair in an upsweep, she waits. Is she surprised when he never comes? When car after car drives by, when headlights appear and recede, while her heart jumps and settles over and over again, until finally it stops bothering, just gives up and lies there in her chest, beating its dull, hopeless patter?

She waits two days before she boards the bus, rides that great distance, and crosses the border. She travels farther still until at last she reaches Victoria and walks through the great oak doors of the Sacred Heart convent. There, she settles in and waits. The nuns are kind, and she likes their pace, their gliding feet and graceful skirts, their grave faces and rough hands.

She's surprised to have a visitor one day, the woman from the opera, the one her father ran off with and married. She is a terribly beautiful woman, Cecily sees, a tall, regal figure with fine bones and translucent skin. In the garden, where they walk below the trees, a top-heavy girl and a woman light as air — bones that seem bird-hollow — Cecily would want to say things to her. Things like, "You killed my mother," and "Everything that has happened to us has been your fault." But she doesn't say them because no one else has been kind to her. No one else has visited, sent a card, said a sympathetic word.

This woman is Beatrice, and she was newly widowed when she met Cecily's father (it was the money, the other sisters say, that made him run off with her). So, this is the trade-off Cecily makes, under the Norfolk pines and the cypresses and the larches. Her mother is gone now; what real difference could it make? And Cecily was always a survivor; she made the best of things.

When the baby is born, she names him Patrick and hands him over to the nuns. Nine pounds lighter, but not appreciably wiser, she walks out the doors of the convent and gets on the next ferry, the tiny one that goes to Salt Spring Island. It's January and cold; the sea is rough and the island looks bleak, the shore stony and cold. There she will learn that you can't walk in the water barefoot, even in the spring and summer, but that there is the most marvelous profusion of hummingbirds that live in the garden and an endless supply of books. She will keep forgetting that the water from the taps is so salty you can't drink it or brush your teeth with it.

She stays for some time with Beatrice and her father, in their house by the sea, the garden that tumbles rockily down to the shore, the kitchen window overlooking it. All season long, things burst and spring and bloom and fade, only to be replaced by something else, equally lovely and surprising.

One by one the letters come, from her scattered sisters. Postmarked from Ottawa and Ohio and even Virginia, her sisters have followed their husbands, their fledgling careers. One becomes an interpreter, one a wife, another gives birth to her own pink babies, four boys in four years' time, and she never looks rested again. But the letters are summarily the same, as though written by the same hand, the same sensibility. They say: How could you? What are you thinking, living there in that house? We don't know if we can ever forgive you. What does Cecily reply to this? Nothing, but she thinks: Well, where were you? How am *I* to forgive you?

But all of this, remember, was before I knew her.

It's the trees that reminded me of that, I suppose, the trees and the cemetery. Walking in the arboretum through this stand of false cypresses—gold thread cypresses, sawara cypresses, golden plume cypresses — and all of them false, according to the yellow tags pinned to their trunks. I was thinking of Cecily and

Beatrice at the convent, chatting awkwardly, filling space with conversation.

But Atilio says, "Not likely."

"What isn't?" I ask.

"You wouldn't find a cypress there, false or otherwise."

"Not the point," I say. But I am irritated with myself, not him. I'm divulging too much, indulging my romantic ideas. Why did I tell him this story?

We walk along the path toward the potter's field; it's buried back here in the arboretum, all but forgotten about. There's a relatively recent marker at the head of it, some scrubby firs, and then a bare, flat field with small stone rectangles, evenly spaced. These are numbered thirty-five, thirty-six, and so forth. Maybe there are fifty of them all together. Early on, he told me that this was deceptive, not true. Really, there are nearly five hundred people buried here, in mass graves. Indigents, he said, I have a list. If you'd like to see it.

I didn't, of course; why would I? But I said I did, and he showed it to me. And now we're walking toward the cemetery with something ahead of us, something that will require this blanket that he carries over one arm.

We meet here when it's nearly dark, after he's closed the gates. It's part of his job — tending to the trees, working in the greenhouse, emptying the trash. I like the way he appears from behind the big waist of a tree, or sneaks up on me when I'm looking around in the twilight, putting his hands on my hips, tugging my hair. I shiver, from the cold and from the feel of his hands. Often this winter, his gloves haven't even come off, and I like that too, the wool on my skin, the added frenzy of finding each other under layers. Almost every part of him is scratchy in some satisfying way or another.

Now it's warming up, mid-March, and I say to him, sitting with our backs against a tree, a blanket pulled up around our chests, "Come spring, we should plant something here. This place is so neglected it depresses me."

He points with his finger to a leaf-covered piece of ground not far away. "Daffodils," he says. "I put them in last season. They'll come up with weeding."

That's nice, I think, and it gives me what I need for today — something about him that makes this worthwhile. I get up and adjust myself, brush the leaves away, the twigs and debris. There is always the smell of compost here, everywhere you walk; it's something like eucalyptus but has a higher pitch, nearer a sound than a scent. "It's time," I say. And just like always, there's no argument from him. He gets up and folds the blanket, stuffs his hands in his pockets. He never touches me afterward or kisses me good-bye. I've never heard his voice on the telephone or seen his handwriting. When I get in the car, he raps the hood twice with his knuckles. See you later.

Of course, Cecily leaves the island eventually and goes on to other things. She tries to become an actress; she works at another radio station; she rescues a Saint Bernard dog that she cannot afford to feed and lives with him in her tiny apartment on the Potomac. She makes friends that she keeps and some she doesn't, and she goes to restaurants where she drinks martinis and eats onion soup. It was the martinis or an entrée, she used to tell me, an easy choice. She all but forgets Walter and Patrick, but she stays in touch with Beatrice, exchanging letters that I've also kept, letters she wrote over the course of years that Beatrice eventually sent to me. Old blue airmail envelopes with that checkered border, tissue-thin sheets of paper ratty with time and reading, tied up with a piece of kitchen twine.

Eventually Cecily gets married; she's almost thirty then. She returns to that town where she was the Lullaby Lady and meets my father on a blind date. What was she doing there? A visit to a sister, perhaps. By now she has made up with two of them; the third never speaks to her again.

My father is a big handsome man in a dull green army uniform. He's charming and has a gift for languages; by the end he will be fluent in five, conversant in several more. He's starting his career in the military, and he talks to Cecily about traveling, seeing the world, driving through Europe in a car with the top down, skiing in Switzerland, sunning in Majorca. Cecily is enthralled; she's still mostly the same girl, still looking for adventure, still intent on living an out-of-the-ordinary life. And what's not to love about James? He has big shoulders and a hundred card tricks; he's solicitous of old ladies and he makes girls blush. He is just inattentive enough to make Cecily wild about him.

They get married at Christ Church; pictures show them shoving cake at each other, frosting mustaches, my mother in a tight wedding suit, looking off-balance, as if her heels are too high. My father mugs for the camera, with that taut, uncomfortable smile he wore whenever he was the center of attention. He is surrounded by his army buddies — slim young men in ill-fitting uniforms, lean-hipped and grinning.

Before long they move to the Middle East, where he works at the embassy. Cecily rescues a big Persian cat and names him Pasha. Things were strict for women, and though she couldn't show any leg in the street, Cecily refused to wear a veil. I was there too, chubby and nearly bald (for the longest time, she said, I was worried). But then a war broke out, a brief one, and we were evacuated, driven in jeeps across the desert. The trip took more than a day, women and children bumping along in open vehicles, young army boys with guns riding along, watching over them. It was so hot, my mother said, hotter than the hinges of hell. And the soldiers, she said, they trained binoculars on the girls and women when they had to get out to go to the bathroom.

"And where's your father?" says Atilio. "While your mother's peeing in the sand dunes?"

"Blowing something up at the embassy, apparently. They had to destroy things — secret documents and so on. So I've been told."

"Now that's interesting." We're in the greenhouse today; the air is nearly tropical. Every time I move, some plant scrapes against my skin. I've shrugged off my sweatshirt, my undershirt; I'm standing there in jeans, my bra, and bare feet, up to my wrists in potting soil. The door is locked though, and the glass so fogged no one could see in.

"Not so rough with the roots," he says to me. "Go a little easy there."

I watch him; he's a medium-sized man with big hands and feet, a hooked nose, a bushy mustache. An expression of deep concentration, one that draws his forehead down around his eyebrows, gives him a glaring, fierce look. But his hands are slow and almost delicate; his fingers never do the wrong thing, never pinch or tear. Beside him, I'm oafish, clumsy. I have no idea what I'm doing. I stand there and wait for instructions, hand him plastic trays or trowels, dig holes in the flecked soil, and let him do the transplanting. He moves the seedlings into the places I've made and tucks them in; I pat down the dirt around them.

"Tell me more about that," he says. "About blowing things up."

I don't know much, so I have to make it up. I tug at my bra strap and manufacture a bridge at midnight, an incendiary device, and a suitcase of secrets. Men setting off explosives and running away, while shots are fired and things—what kind of things?—explode. "But, that's all I know," I tell him. "It's classified."

"Neat," he says, and pats my behind.

Here, in this humid space, I'm remarkably tolerant. The hot green scent, our rough hands, the unshaven face that rubs mine, the dirt I need to wash away at the end of it. The trips to the store for milk—are you bathing in it? my husband says; the dirt under my fingernails—grubbing around in the garden again? he says. Yes, I say, to all of it. The itch of the dirt and the soft, sighing, sleepy clean of the bathtub—that's what I'm after.

Now Atilio says, "I bought butter for you, earlier."

"What for?" I stare at him over a potting table, some baby green thing—what will it grow up to be?—dangling from my trying-to-be-careful fingers.

"Thought I'd save you a trip to the store."

Thank you, I tell him. But I think, how did he know this? Have I told him what I do on the way home, stop for some unremarkable grocery item—just in case Mark is home early, asks where I've been? I can't remember but reach for my shirt, hanging on a nail by a big-fingered fern. I shrug it on. I stand there, dressed, waiting for him to say something else, something like "Don't go so soon," but of course he doesn't. My shoes are all that's left. I'll slip them on before I go out the door, scuff downhill to my car, parked in a tucked-away spot, hidden by huge hills of wood shavings.

"Next time," he says, when I'm opening the heavy door, just as the real air hits my face, cools me off, "Next time bring me a picture of something."

I walk away in the falling light. There's a half-cup of moon overhead, nearly transparent, like it was cut from the same cloth as the clouds. I see oceans and mountain ranges and all the moon's continents, shifting and closing in on each other.

———

I walk in the arboretum because the dog got hit by a car. Last spring he got away from me and went galloping into the road. I saw it happen. I used to bring him here every day. I just kept coming.

Now I'm learning the trees, trying to identify the ones that aren't marked. There's a strange mixture, native trees and imports, those odd, acid-yellow cypresses, the Japanese larch, the Canada hemlock. "Is it like a Canada goose?" I ask him. "A Canada hemlock, rather than a Canadian one?"

"Beats me," he says. He's not a big talker, this man, not a great intellectual. But I have enough of that at home. There I have a psychologist, an analyzer of motives, a head-scratcher. He's like hot breath in my face, all the time.

Atilio and I have never made a single plan or arrangement. I don't know where he lives or what he eats, which side of the bed he prefers, whether or not he is allergic to cats. I come or I don't, sometimes three times a week, sometimes not at all, and he never looks disappointed or slighted. He could be married too, for all I know.

Today he's dusting the rhododendrons in the memorial garden, spraying them white with pesticide. I'm sitting on a rock, my legs drawn up, thinking that soon I'll be wearing shorts and that I inherited this terrible, unfashionable paleness from both of them. Atilio is dark, just this side of swarthy, and when he touches my freckles he laughs, says I'm carpeted with them. I can look down at myself, at his finger connecting dots, and deny this with a nearly straight face.

I want to tell him about the affair she had when we lived in Turkey. For obvious reasons, this is on my mind. I look at him and find he's watching me a little, with the spray bottle in his hand, crouching down. "Come here," he says, and I do.

I wonder if she felt this way — felt simple and desired. Like a spider waiting quietly for movement, neither hungry nor restless, in the kind of trance you'd like to hold forever.

The best picture of Cecily shows her shoulders and waspish waist; she's dressed for a party, in a shiny sleeveless dress that might be black or blue. She's half-shrugging, with a wide smile on her face and her hair coiled at her neck. The best picture of my father has him seated on the edge of a chair, in profile, a cigarette in one hand, a deck of cards in the other. Both pictures are in black and white, and I've put them together in the same frame, on that huge piano, though they don't really belong.

They were always in a rush, the two of them, off to a dance or a dinner, sweeping in to say good night in a cloud of Arpege and pipe tobacco, her jewelry brushing my cheek, his sharp cuff against my shoulder. They were glamorous, always a little tipsy and loud.

What I've done is this: I've taken the letters and the pictures and ordered them together. They make their own sort of sense, the obvious, like the age I was when they were taken, but there are other less evident meanings. When we lived in Turkey, for example, the pictures and the letters change. In the letters, she asks Beatrice: "What am I to do?" These correspondences are stiff; they seem coded, full of something understood but un-inked. The pictures tell a different tale; in them, she looks younger than she has in years. She even looks taller, shoulders drawn up and squared, smiling all the time. You see her lover in some of these as well, and the way she is aware of him even when she is not looking in his direction. There's something coursing there between them, and I imagine that the right sort of film could have captured it, like a photograph in which something ghostly, or paranormal, appears. It would look like lines of current, a singeing sort of heat.

I was nearly ten then, with tight pigtails and a line of chalk-white scalp, thick glasses that I hated, and a concave stomach I remember fondly. The horse was named Black Velvet; the Turkish for that is nearly unpronounceable. Ahmet was an ex-cavalry man, straight-spined and white-haired, his face etched by the sun, always smiling. He said: heels down, hands soft, seat fastened to saddle. He made a soft, chirping sound in his mouth, talking to horses; it meant hush now, and hurry up. He taught me to ride standing up, to do tricks, spinning around on a moving animal's back, hands on a sursaddle. This is balance, he said; the rest comes later.

The day he put her in the saddle, I stood and watched, green-eyed, hanging on a fence rail. I saw his hand touch her thigh, stroke the line of her lower back and her haunch, showing her where things belonged. She looked down at him, awkward up there — looking foolish, I thought — and smiled. I noticed then, quite suddenly, that she was beautiful, something that had been hidden from me before.

Other people must have noticed the attention he paid her, the special lessons and time. There was a trailer parked near the entrance to the stable, and they disappeared into it for what seemed like hours, though I know now it couldn't have been. It must have been time snatched and wolfed down, like mine here.

In particular I remember one overnight ride in the summer. The whole stable went along, all of us packed and burdened, like we were off on a crusade or a campaign of war. Sleeping bags and cooking utensils, food for us and the horses, a destination it would take all day to reach. They rode together at the head of the group. Her seat was better by then, and she rode with one hand on her thigh, bouncing slightly, easy up there.

The land spread out and lay down, gentle hills and scruffy vegetation, a tremendous dustiness that made the horses blow and snort. I rode with the older girls, girls who played games with boys in the hayloft, girls who smoked cigarettes and groomed their horses obsessively. They never asked me about Cecily, about Ahmet, but they knew. I saw it in the looks they exchanged, the giggles, and the way they could gesture with their eyes, their fingers light on the braided reins.

Late that night, when the ride was done — the marshmallows blackened, the stars winking down, sleeping bags unrolled and waiting — my mother found me. She had decided not to sleep outdoors with us, she said, at the last minute, as everyone arranged their tack, patted their animals good night. The air was cool and clear, smoke-tinged, and filled with the sound of tired horses, a huff of air, a nicker. She pointed, over there, a low building like a barrack, a single bedroom. I'm too old for this, she told me. I'm taking the bed.

But I couldn't sleep. I was crazy with it, with catching her, with showing her to herself. I crouched near the window of the building, waiting for him. I imagined her inside, on that narrow cot, warm and hopeful. What might I have done? I had no plan. Anyway, Ahmet never came. He never slipped around the building on cat feet, never turned the doorknob of that room. Near daylight, sick to my stomach with nerves and disappointment, I slid into my sleeping bag, slept fitfully until the sounds woke me, until I felt her hand on my shoulder, her bright voice saying, "Up we go, sleepyhead." I nearly fell off my horse, on that long ride back, my eyes closing, the rock of the horse and the creak of the saddle like a kind of lullaby.

"So there was another way in," says Atilio now, sounding certain.

"I'm sure of it," I say, but am I? I was only ten, after all; I must have been easy to sidestep, to trick. But then, too, I had a wild imagination; I read Gothic romances, slim paperbacks with lurid covers.

Now he's holding this picture, taken at a party they had. She's dancing with Ahmet, in a black sweater with silver ribbing on the sleeves, their fingers touching lightly, miles of decorous space between them. They're laughing at each other, and I see my father in the background, smiling at them.

"He didn't know?" says Atilio, and he touches a finger to my mother's hair, longer then, still shiny, serpent-thick.

I lift my shoulders, shrug. "I doubt it." I have my hand on his wrist, one finger tapping his knuckle. I'm bare-armed, in jeans and boots, leaning against his truck. I'm making a study of his mouth, the way it changes its mind, curves and thins, the pout that might, on another face, be girlish.

"Can I keep this?" he says, rubbing the edges, still staring at it.

"Why?" I'm not certain about this, not at all. I've been careful to leave nothing behind, but he's never asked me for a thing before and it's not my favorite. I say, "I guess. If you want." Not so generous, not very gracious at all.

This doesn't faze him; he leans in the open window of the truck and tucks the picture under the sun visor.

"I'll take you home," he says, and what he means is he'll walk me to my car. When we get there, he opens the back door to show me what he's done— filled the backseat with daffodils and hydrangea, a tall amaryllis in a basket, pots of tulips with feathered petals. I touch his face and he pulls away a little, nervous about being seen, though the parking lot is empty.

"There was a sale last weekend," he says. "I would have had to throw them all away. Compost."

I smile at him because I'm glad for this. I don't want gifts from his heart, gestures that could be interpreted by me, that might keep me up at night.

Still I say, "How romantic. Thank you."

When I'm backing away, leaving him there, he calls after me, "Bring the basket back from the amaryllis. I like to keep those."

Driving home, I'm overwhelmed by the scent; in the enclosed car it's close and almost noxious. Funereal. It turns my stomach, and I do what I would have done anyway, pull over on a side street and get out, carry pots and tubs to the curb, held in my fingers, two by two. I almost forget, but then I go back, pick up the amaryllis by its tough stalk, and pull the wicker basket away from it, dragging roots and soil. There is a tearing noise as it comes free, and I drop it on the ground, put the basket in the trunk. Somewhere near home I realize that I must have planted some of these myself weeks ago, that he and I had babied them along in the greenhouse, working silently, side by side. That our fingers, carrying traces and scents of each other, had buried these things, wished them well.

The letters came to me in a small cedar box, the kind made by Sears thirty-odd years ago. The pictures I've always had, some jammed in an old shoebox, some glued into albums, cataloged with Cecily's neat handwriting. This is something I've been putting off for a while, and Mark is mildly surprised when he comes home and finds them spread out on the piano, letters divorced from envelopes, pictures piled by decade, by country. I'm fastening photographs to letters with paper clips, making a story that I can understand. Mapping her life in her own words, layering them with her expressions, her endless hairstyles.

Beatrice is in many of these pictures, always the ones with Christmas trees, or scenes of snow and gray streets. After Cecily's father died, she came every Christmas, to whatever country we were living in, bringing gifts for me, cosmetics for Cecily, books and tobacco for my father. Did Beatrice know that she cost Cecily her relationship with her oldest sister? Would she have cared? I doubt it. She was the same woman Cecily must have met under the trees years earlier, with a ramrod posture and sharp tweed suits. She was always willowy and aloof. She carried herself like a ship, tall and proud, capable of parting things, of traveling on fragile surfaces.

When she and Cecily were together once a year, they whispered and spoke softly, said aloud all the things they must have intimated in their correspondence. At times, Cecily's letters to her were a little frantic; they seemed written by a nervous woman, one on the brink of something dire. Looking at them now, I wonder why. Surely there was no possibility of Ahmet's leaving his wife; she was terribly ill, confined to a wheelchair. And Cecily, she was a military wife — could she really have left my father, lived with a foreign man in his country, where she wouldn't have had the privileges of being an American? The access to maids and houseboys, to electricity when others went without, to medical care?

Motherhood, she thought, was a lark. It was play a game, sing a song, where's the sitter? Is it my fault I took my childhood more seriously?

But maybe I'm being stingy. Could she have done something grand for love? Or was the tone in her letters no more than you might expect, the desperation of impossible circumstances, of a certain satisfying hopelessness? Or another explanation, that I interpreted her letters the same way I listened to her speak, thinking she was overwrought, too caught up in herself — too uninterested in me.

When I was older, we got to be friends, the kind of uneasy friendship we could achieve by pretending that a great number of things never happened. She came to visit me once; I was living with some boyfriend, there was a holiday involved, and I had something I wanted to ask her about. It had been bothering me for some time, and to bring it up I had to admit that I'd been snooping, looking around in her dresser drawers for something. "Stockings," she said to me at the time, in that cramped living room. She was fingering the stem of her wineglass, looking small and curled at the end of a sofa. "You were always taking my stockings."

"Maybe," I said, but I might just have been having a look around. I was always trying to figure her out, wanting to know her secrets, thinking there must be a key somewhere, like a legend on a map. The paper was folded very small, brown and crackling with age, a roughness that made you think it had been much handled, seams splitting at the fold.

I found it years ago, but it took me a while to get around to asking her. She didn't invite personal questions. People who pry, she told me once, deserve whatever they find. And aren't entitled to an explanation. What I found was Patrick's birth certificate, and I had studied it in confusion, standing over her dresser in the dim light of her bedroom, her silver mirror that rattled when you held it and the matching hairbrush laid carefully on a piece of lace-edged fabric. It had not been what I was looking for; it had not even been something I'd considered. So I returned it, thoughtfully, between her folded lingerie, under the rubbery fake breast she wore after the mastectomy.

There was a stretch of time before she spoke, and then all she said was, "Oh, that."

We looked at each other. I could hear the boyfriend in the other room, tidying something.

"Aren't you interested in what happened to him?" I knew she wasn't. It wouldn't have been like her, but the question begged asking.

"I'm not," she said predictably. "And nor should you be."

That was the end of it as far as she was concerned. It wasn't much my business as she saw it. Maybe she was right. So we went on, spoke of other things and cooked a meal together. We made that holiday phone call to Margaret, the sister she still kept in touch with. There was one down now, to pneumonia two years earlier, and there was the oldest, still in Ottawa, whom I had never met because Cecily and she were both too stubborn to mend fences. We spoke to Margaret and her children; we laughed about some things, promised to speak soon.

I put her on a train the next day, unsatisfied but not much surprised, and watched her go. She and my father were long divorced, not due to any affair of hers in particular, or any restlessness, but to a general weariness on Cecily's part, some instinct that made her leave one Sunday afternoon when I was in college and not come back. She lived in a small townhouse with an orange cat, and she kept on riding horses, made close women friends, and seemed, for a time, quite uncharacteristically happy.

What I learned about Ahmet surprised me. Margaret told me about it, not long ago. We left Turkey for the States; it would be our last overseas post. I remember little about the departure, the move, although there must have been a scene or two, good-byes and tears and promises. They wrote letters for a long time, Margaret said, kept up a sad, secret correspondence. Then she told me this: that Cecily wrote to him, not long after she became ill, and told him about it. And that she never heard from him again. Not a word, Margaret said. Not a blessed word.

Margaret told me this in her house in Ohio, over coffee, showing me pictures of Cecily back then — those hairstyles, those eyebrows! We had taken Cecily to Ohio to be buried next to her mother, and the other sister came in from Ottowa, the one I'd never known. They hadn't spoken in thirty years, but she came to the funeral. She looked shockingly like Cecily, her figure and face, the way she put a finger on her lower lip, her hands and the wrinkles around her eyes. I wanted to be close to her for this reason only, to touch and study her, discover her secrets, as if they might have been anything like Cecily's.

All I really know is what I've been told by Margaret, what I've read, and what I see in photographs. Not enough to go on, not nearly. As if Cecily were a mathematical equation to be solved, as if the answer might be simple and perfect. In truth, everything I've said is just speculation, fancy knitting.

———

In the potter's field, the daffodils are coming up, pushing through soil and dead leaves, looking green and hopeful. I'm clearing space for them, gently, pushing debris aside. It's warm and I'm kneeling on my jacket. There is broken glass around; teenagers must have found this place, and now they come to drink beer, do other things. We pick it up, Atilio and I, prying up amber shards, but it's a losing battle. Several days ago a new marker appeared, a wide bright stone, laid flat, freshly cut. Willie S. Gardner, it reads, beloved Gramma.

"What's this?" I asked him. I was unsettled by it — displeased, territorial.

"Some people came by looking for the list," he told me. "Their grandmother is here. They put in the stone. Last week, I think."

I thought about this for a minute, remembered what he had told me about this place. "How did they know where to put it?"

"No way to tell," he said. "It's such a huge muddle. Disorganized. They just picked a spot, stuck it there."

"There's something about that I hate," I said. "Don't you?"

"Not really my business," he said. "I told them, do what you want."

Now I sit back and scratch my scalp, tug my hair through my fingers. I smell him on my hands as they pass my face; I bring them back to find it again. There's something about the smell of a man that can make you remember why you loved him, if you've had enough time to forget it. Sometimes minutes are all you need.

But there's something else different here, other than that new, thrown-anywhere stone, the glass, an aerosol container of something. The land is lying differently now, the last patchy snow gone, the leaves stepped on and sunken so that the real shape of this place has emerged from winter. I see what it is, suddenly. The ground sinks in even depressions, one and two feet deep, end to end and across the entire field. Graves, like secrets, are rising to the surface, or the ground itself is sinking down to meet them, bear them up.

"God," I say to him. "Look at that."

He nods. "Yep," he says. "You bet."

I look around. The land rocks, dipping and rising, hard breasts and hips of earth. Graves, I see now, and nothing else. They are reproachful, something I should have noticed long ago, when I made noises in their wells, got up and dusted bones from my back.

"What bothers you?" I ask him now, because nothing seems to, nothing at all.

"My paycheck," he says. "Aphids. Root rot."

"I'm pregnant," I tell him.

His hands keep working, sure and gentle. His eyes are on mine but his fingers brush leaves, pluck at twigs. There's a sheen on his forehead, stubble on his chin. He sits up, transfers his hands to his knees, rubs at them.

"Really?" he says. I still can't tell, can't see what he's thinking.

"Maybe not," I tell him. "Not for sure."

"Well," he says. "That's something."

"Probably I'm not," I say. "Just late."

"Okay," he says and gets to his feet, dusts his hands. "I'll walk you back. I have a Chinese dogwood to put in, out by the shag forest."

Walking back through the woods, he touches my hand, just brushes the back of my wrist with his. We're not looking at each other; there's no need. There's that electricity, hair on skin; it's there and then gone, leaving a coolness, a near ache.

Some months ago he told me about the shag forest. We were in it but I didn't know — it's only a stretch of dead trees in a living forest, broken limbs, splintered and pale as bone, dry bark, no kind of shelter from the sky. But no, he told me then, it's very much alive. Like a housing development now, but the houses are dead. The trees keep standing because things are making a home in them, burrowing, nesting, and being born. Listen, he said. And then, standing there quietly, you could almost hear it — the rustle of living things, the busyness of growth, of endless breeding and foraging.

There's nothing else to tell him; I've said all I know. But I am Cecily's daughter; I've been telling stories, pressing up against the microphone, listening to the sound of my own voice. Is this what

Cecily learned? That if you let yourself look, it's so easy to see what people don't want to know. Cecily knew that about me, I think — that all my questions were just another way of saying, don't tell me. Let me guess and fumble, but keep your secrets; keep them cool and close and bury them deep.

Glazing

Today, there is no room for mistakes. But from
the start there are glitches, unanticipated wrenches she couldn't
have accounted for. First, it is raining sheets, straight vertical curtains of water that show no sign of easing. Next, Lila puts her arm
through a pane in the bedroom window while trying to let in
some air. There is a popping sound as her hand goes through, and
she stands there, amazed, while large triangular shards fall onto
the bookshelf and into the front yard. Rainwater collects rapidly
in her open palm. Around her wrist are perilously sharp points of
glass, and she thinks, as she twists her hand to draw it back inside
the house, how perfectly designed each one is to open a vein, or
an artery. She wipes her rain-soaked hand on her pajamas and

studies the damage. Where, at this hour, in this weather, and on a Sunday, no less, will she find a glazier? The house is old, is the problem. They, she and Rich, haven't been able to get it together lately; the house has seemed the least of their worries. The roof needs redoing, certainly, and people seem to notice that the up-stairs is on a definite slant, that there is a small ski slope between the two upper bedrooms.

Watching people troop through her house, with their sharp, critical comments, their dismissive scrutiny, has been surprising. These were not things Lila had ever noticed or thought prohibi-tive. She thinks her failing is an almost pathological ability to overlook the obvious. Once she would have called it seeing be-yond the difficulties; now she realizes that it is not so quaint as that, and far less romantic. Lila, buying the house several years before, had been immediately taken by its charm — the exposed beams, the balcony looking down into the living room, the im-mense stone fireplace. She had made an offer while standing in the kitchen, seized suddenly by fear, afraid that someone might take it from her while she dawdled with details, with engineers and inspectors. Had she investigated, she'd have found that the house had been on the market for nearly a year, that there was an abandoned oil tank on the property, that it sat both in wetlands and a flood plain.

She finishes drying her hand on the corner of the bedspread and then straightens it, as though a well-made bed might dis-tract from a broken window, from the rain that is now splattering the bookshelf beneath it and dripping down onto the floorboards. She goes to the bathroom for a towel. While there, she decides to empty the medicine cabinet and the two drawers that hold her makeup. She fills the wastebasket with nubs of old lipstick tubes, with broken powder compacts and unused lotions, empty bottles of antibiotics, her diaphragm, a rusted eyelash curler. Her hands turn suntan brown from the powder; it cakes the creases of her palm. When had she hoped to use such a shade, when her skin is so fair, so opposed to sunlight?

Rich is calling her name. She hears the loud sound of his foot-steps on the old floors, imagines him coming along through the house, ducking through the low doorways automatically.

"I'm here," she calls. She turns on the water and scrubs at her palm. The faucets are reversed, hot right and cold left, which these astute house-shoppers unfailingly notice, and she wonders if there's time to switch them.

"Jesus God," he says, and she remembers the window. "What the hell?"

"That was the strangest thing," she says, coming out of the bathroom. "It just fell right out."

He is, as he always points out, far too large of a man for this house. Lila's hobbit house, he used to call it. Lately: this goddam sardine tin. His shoulders are at the height of the bank of windows; he keeps his head tucked into his neck, nearly all the time. The bedroom, which had seemed neat and perfectly sized when she lived here alone, now feels cramped and ridiculous.

"That's fabulous," he says. His back is still toward her; his hand plays in the amoebalike gathering of water on the bookshelf. "That's just tremendous. Do you know that the stream is also considering coming inside? Maybe these people would like to snorkel through. I'll call and ask."

"Cover it," Lila tells him. She goes to the closet and finds a pair of jeans. She rifles the shelves for a sweatshirt. She finds an old one of her mother's; the cuffs are shredded and the tears across the chest grow with each washing. "Should I make muffins or something, for the smell?"

"What do you suggest I cover it with? Couldn't you just not touch anything until we sell this dump?"

"It was an accident. Did I not mention that?" Lila pushes past him and leaves the room. She is thinking of a package of blueberries she had seen in the refrigerator, what was it, a week ago? Even if they aren't still good, she could make prop muffins, to fill the house with that baking smell.

The kitchen clock says noon. She loads the counter with flour and butter, sugar, sour cream, the furry blueberries. She hears Rich swearing in the bedroom — the house really is that small. While she works, he passes her several times, carrying large pieces of cardboard, duct tape, a utility knife.

As he went by once she said to him, "People tend to notice houses with cardboard windows."

He made no sign he'd heard.

When the muffins are in the oven, she stands at the counter

and looks into the backyard. He's right, the stream is closing in on the French doors; the grass is inches underwater, and green shafts poke up as if seeking air. The water rushes downward, making its way through a cleft in the rocks, gathering speed as it ducks under the curved footbridge, and then roaring over the little fall into the rock-edged pond. The rhododendrons have dropped their glistening petals onto the grass. Through the trees she sees the property marker fluttering in the wind; it's a length of Mylar party streamer they had tacked up a few weeks ago, when prospective buyers couldn't read the survey map.

The couple they are expecting today are what the realtor calls "on the hook." This is their third time to the house. Lila doesn't much like them, but she's given up on her original fantasy — giving the house over to some nice people who would appreciate its history, the master stonework, its quirky charm. The husband of this couple rides a motorcycle. He has the entire Harley Davidson wardrobe; he wears his keys on his waist on a length of chain. The wife is mousy and sour; she's not interested in the house's antique status or that it's in the historical register. She wants to know where the manuals are for the appliances, what are the dimensions of the closets.

In the lower pond, the duck family is swirling around in circles. Paddling madly against the surprisingly strong current, the male is making annoyed noises, lifting out of the water and shaking his feathers.

Rich comes into the kitchen, drying his hands on his thighs. He says, "Bird feeders draw rodents."

Lila takes the muffins from the oven. They look good, they smell fine, there is no evident furriness. She shakes them into a basket.

"Take it down if you want."

"I intend to."

When did they begin talking to one another like this? And if they had noticed it, nipped it right there, would things have deteriorated this far? Much as she searches pockets of herself for remembered feelings, for kindnesses and charities that surely once existed, she comes up empty. Now, sometimes, if she questions him about it, he will say something deliberately loathsome. He'll say, "Oh, I do love you Lila. Lovey, lovey, lovey." He'll say it in a hateful voice, a playground voice, one that makes her skin crawl. Strange how it could come to this with no precipitating event — no infidelity or betrayal, nothing like that. Just a grinding down of affection, of tolerance, until even the smallest allowances seem too extraordinary, too far beyond them.

Now she says, "I might have cut myself badly on that window. There's a scratch. You could have asked."

"If you had, I'm sure you would have let me know."

"What's that supposed to mean?"

He is silent for a moment. "When you're unhappy, Lila, everyone knows it. Never fear."

Lila stares at him. The room pulses with unsaid things — all for the good, probably. She is surprised by their unforeseen capacity for violence, the way her fingers sometimes clench with the desire to strike out at him — to bite, or scratch or stab — a look she sees on his face as well and finds strangely exciting. The effort, sometimes, to step back from the edge of those feelings leaves her exhausted — frustrated and aroused. The house is a dangerous place these days, a minefield.

Lila's mother, near the end, had become a woman with a dark and bawdy sense of humor. This cancer, she would say to Lila, is killing me. In good health she had been a guarded, conservative woman; she admonished Lila not to get above herself, or ahead of herself. But later, when things were dire, she lightened up considerably. She had an entourage of nurses for a time, and Lila, visiting for a weekend, would step into the house on tiptoe, expecting some grim, deathly scene, only to find them all gathered on her mother's bed, painting each other's toenails, telling filthy stories. It was unseemly, and Lila's efforts to turn the room's conversation back to talk of medications and bathroom visits would be met with blank looks or fits of giggling. They were like schoolgirls caught at some mischief. Lila was aware, through much of her mother's illness, that the smile she wore could best be described as pained.

"Sit down," Lila's mother said once. "Let me tell you a story."

Lila, cautious and uneasy, did as she was told. Her mother was having a good day; the bedside lamp was lit, the newspaper was spread across the bed, and the big orange cat sprawled in its center.

"Remember I said that Greg visited? A month or so ago?"

Lila nodded. She remembered Greg from childhood, the husband of one of her mother's friends — a woman who had tried to teach Lila Spanish once and had also secretly taught her mother to drive. This was the kind of story Lila expected. Perhaps even the same one, about how they had taken the car out when the husbands had been away and then Lila's mother had parallel-parked into the driver's side of Greg's car. Her mother was taking a lot of pills at the time; stories tended to repeat.

"So, he was here. He and Alison are divorced, you knew that? For years. He doesn't have the mustache anymore. He looks much better, but he's still short. Anyway he spent the night because, well, it just made sense at the time. We had a nice dinner; he got Chinese food at the place in the mall. By the A&P, you know the one."

Lila, sitting at the edge of the bed, was surreptitiously reading an article in the Entertainment section about a celebrity divorce. She said, "Uh-huh."

"I was asleep; God knows what time it was. He was in the guest room down the hall. So, suddenly I feel this pressure on the bed, near where you're sitting now. And you know what a light sleeper I am."

Do I ever, Lila thought, remembering her teenage years and all of her discovered escapades.

"So he says to me, Anne, he says, I have always wanted to make love to you. And now here we are, both of us alone, both divorced. Can I get under the covers?"

Lila looked up sharply. She searched her mother's face for signs that this was a joke of some kind, a tasteless joke. But her mother was nodding a little, and the smile she was wearing was not the teasing kind. "That's what I said," she told Lila. "You heard correctly."

Lila caught, for a moment, the whiff of illness that surrounded her mother, that she had become accustomed to. A scent not unlike dying flowers, cloying, but not entirely offensive. Her mother was not wearing her wig; her scalp was stippled with dark fuzz —

the doctors had stopped the chemo finally, mercifully. Her face was sunken, but her skin had become oddly lovely, translucent even. Under the covers, Lila knew that her mother's body was wasted. She knew because she turned away when she had to help her bathe and that she would think up almost any excuse not to do it, not to have to look. Her remaining breast was grotesquely long, the scar beside it savage; it looked to Lila as if she had been the victim of a wartime amputation, with no thought whatsoever given to cosmetics. Her legs, always thin, now seemed too scrawny to support her; her stomach was pouched and flaccid above a child's hairless pubis.

"Good God," Lila said. She stroked the cat; she pictured her mother's naked body; she tried to conjure this scene.

"What's wrong pussycat? Too gruesome to imagine?" Her mother was examining her face, and Lila realized then that it was a private joke of some kind, a test, a tease.

"You're always trying to get a rise out of me, aren't you?" Lila stood up and shook the cat off the papers. She folded them noisily.

"Maybe." Her mother lay back against the pillows and closed her eyes. "It's true though, every word of it. Hit the light on your way out, will you?"

At the door Lila paused; she dug her toes into the carpet, tapped her nails on the doorjamb. "What happened?" she asked, in spite of herself.

Her mother laughed. "What do you think? I sent him away of course. I mean, look at me. Well, no need to tell you. Just look at your face."

Lila, describing her mother to the few people now interested who never met her, has only good things to say. Funny, she recounts, quirky. These days, she's noticed, people like to think of their mothers as characters — eccentric, slightly flawed, full of humor and high jinks. There is a version of Lila's mother that can be wrestled credibly into this sort of a person. Even Rich says, *Gosh, I wish I'd met her.* For a time, when they were first together, he had even had a moony relationship with a picture of

Lila's mother, a particularly flattering photograph taken when she was roughly Lila's age. In it, her mother has an old-fashioned sort of glamour, a shiny evening frock, a provocative smile. That the picture is black and white goes a distance toward this impression; you imagine cigarette holders and pillbox hats, champagne parties and evening gloves. Rich was taken with it, and this pleased Lila, to think that she might have had that sort of mother. It was nearly enough that he thought so.

That photograph, at the moment, is packed in a box with a number of others — with baby photos of Lila and other things of her mother's she cannot bear to throw away. Two stacked boxes are beneath the piano, which blocks the house's original front door; it is too short for even Lila to use comfortably. Now they enter the house through a mudroom, painted a rich hunter's red; she has tried to transform it into an entryway of sorts, with pictures and floral arrangements.

Rich is standing in the rain, feeding the ducks. He's feeding them blueberry muffins, which he claimed smelled spoiled and took outside before the buyers arrived. Still, she thought, the house had been sugary and warm. It had gone fairly well, the realtor had said so. She warned, though, that they will likely have to bring the price down again; they have brought it down already three times. And the realtor, who had first suggested this tentatively, has now taken off the kid gloves. She seems to enjoy pointing out the house's defects, and her manner with Lila is much less deferential.

"She's sick of us," Lila had said to Rich when everyone had left, after they had congratulated each other on the patch job on the window, which had passed unnoticed.

"Well," Rich had said, "Who isn't?"

Lila opens the French doors and walks outside. She slogs through the grass to the edge of the pond and positions herself on a mossy rock. "Who'll feed the ducks when we're gone?"

"We're not the first people to think of feeding ducks, I imagine."

"Still. We should say something."

"Good idea. We can have it as a clause in the contract."

"God," she says, "this is miserable."

"Well, probably these people will buy it and then we can be done. Adiós and arrivederci."

"I meant the rain," says Lila, untruthfully, perversely. The look on his face says he's not a bit fooled.

At the end they'd moved Lila's mother to the hospital. There was no false hope this time, no thinking she'd go home again. Afternoons, Lila sat in a fake leather armchair with sloping wooden arms and read magazines. Her mother drifted, disoriented, in a haze of narcotics. She seemed to be remembering things that had happened years ago, people now long gone, names Lila only vaguely recognized. At Lila's feet was a bottle of wine she had smuggled in; she longed for a cigarette, a morphine drip of her own.

The nurses didn't bother her; the doctor stopped by infrequently, arranging her face into a grave expression of sympathy. Lila thought she ought to be making a scene — wasn't that what was done? She should demand experimental drugs and treatments; she should bully the nurses and insist on answers from the doctors. Instead she was lulled by the quiet noise of the hospital corridors, the way the lights dimmed after hours and only bluish fluorescents flickered and hummed above the nurses' station. There was the sound of wheels passing, the noise of machines, the distant pinging of the elevator reaching the floor.

Below the windows, lights arched over the parking lot. She could see her mother's car down there, four rows over and seven back; she could just see the curve of the red hood. When she left the hospital to drive home again, she would own that car and the contents of her mother's house. At some moments — mostly when an orderly or a nurse stepped into the room — Lila felt like a restaurant patron who has lingered too long over coffee; she felt hustled and rude. She imagined lines of patients with hopes of recovery waiting in the corridors, checking their watches, tapping their heels. This was why the smiles she gave the nurses were conciliatory and slightly abashed, why she felt, privately, as though they were united. She felt a strange affinity for them — for their soft efficiency, their willingness to touch the untouchable, the ugly, the dying. Her mother, in her stupor, was as oblivious as she'd been her entire life, as unaware of people's feelings and needs — like when she'd served a bloody roast to Lila's vegetarian boyfriend, a thing Lila was certain she'd done deliberately, to broadcast her opinion that not eating meat was silly, an affectation. She'd enjoyed embarrassing Lila; sometimes this had seemed to border on malice. On that occasion, she'd ratcheted it up a notch by insisting that the boyfriend carve; she'd run her finger around the rim of the platter and brought the red juices to her lips with a coy, carnivorous smile.

From the phone in the corridor, Lila left a message for her married boyfriend. He was on a trip with his wife, on some island vacation with casinos and sparkling beaches. It had been a subject of mild contention between them, but Lila was keenly aware of her role in the relationship. She was not entitled to argue with him. He was more than her boyfriend; he was also her boss. The relationship was so uneven, so grossly skewed, that Lila did not even have the will to extricate herself from it. She thought, with equivalent horror, of the two possibilities — that he wouldn't leave his wife and that he might.

A nurse shook Lila awake when he returned the call; Lila picked up the phone at the nurses' station.

"This had better be serious," he said.

"She's dying," Lila told him. "I need you to come." She turned her back on the nurses. She heard the plaintive note in her voice; she was certain of the power those words held. She felt a surge of leverage, heady and unfamiliar.

"Come on, Lila, she'll be fine." His voice crackled through the line; she pictured him standing on a balcony under the Southern Cross, drinking black sambuca, smoking a cigar.

"I'm not exaggerating here. This is it. The doctor's said so." She hadn't exactly, not in so many words.

"Christ," he said. "This is incredibly inconvenient. I can't just go jetting out of here on a moment's notice."

"That's fine," said Lila. "Don't worry about it." She hung on the end of the phone, waiting, knowing she should hang up.

"I'll send someone," he said finally, "to give you a hand."

He had, amazingly, done just that. He'd sent his lawyer, a big Hungarian man with an unpronounceable last name. He had rumpled clothes and badly cut hair; he got to work immediately, pushing people around.

Nonetheless, her mother's breathing grew shallow and more labored; her chest heaved. Her eyes were closed; her hands were folded on her stomach, on top of the bedclothes. Tom, the lawyer, looked helpless. He wanted to know when Lila had last eaten or slept. He took the wine away and disposed of the bottle. Finally he went away and came back; he'd arranged for Lila to sleep in the nurses' room down the hall. For a few hours, he said; you look like hell. Only if you come lie down with me, she told him.

In the dark room, he eased himself onto the cot beside her. He kept inches between them; when she put her arms around him he stiffened. He was big and warm; he was an armchair, a soft blanket. Lila moved her hands around his chest; she slid them under his wrinkled cotton shirt; she fingered the hairs on his soft belly. Go to sleep, he said. She thought of kissing him, and tried. He pulled away, lifting his head and resting his chin on her nose. She kept at him, touching, prodding, nestling. He said, I have a job I'd like to keep. In her head, Lila heard her mother's painful breathing; she imagined she could hear it through the walls. If she touched her hand to it, she might feel the chain-stoking against her palm. Each breath was excruciating, endless; each one was surely the last.

The lawyer pulled away; she pulled him back. She ran her sock feet along his pant's leg, up against his shinbone. She climbed on top of him and moved her body on his; she took the skin of his neck in her mouth. She held him by handfuls, in increments, one piece of flesh at a time. Minutes ticked by, hours passed. He resisted her; they struggled.

Outside the room, the nurses changed shifts. The one who went home didn't bother to tell the new one where Lila was. When they came out later, orderlies had taken her mother's body away; they were changing the sheets. Lila was aware of how they looked, how rumpled and undone: her hair was ratty, her shirt was crumpled, she'd lost a sock. The nurses slid their eyes past; they focused on the forms that needed filling out. They poured into Lila's hand the cold, slithering length of chain that had been around her mother's neck. A folded pile of clothes: a torn sweatshirt and loose pants, a pair of tiny tennis shoes, ankle socks.

Driving home to her mother's house, she passed bars she had been drunk in, late-night restaurants she and her friends had tumbled into after hours, looking for eggs and trouble, for Bloody Marys that would carry them into morning, to daylight, to brunch. She stopped for a pack of cigarettes, combed her fingers through her hair, swiped lipstick at her mouth. She rode the whole way sitting on the square red cushion that her mother had used to lift herself up so she could see over the dash.

At the house, the cat was frantic with intuition, with feline perception. He prowled around her legs, howling. When she lay down in her mother's bed, smelling Arpege and orange night cream, he ranged up and down her body, kneading angrily.

There had been a faint rain falling in the hospital parking lot; it showed under the lights, making the asphalt slick and black. There was a glow at the edge of the sky, over the river. The lawyer shook her hand.

He said: It's Lila, right? I'm very sorry for your loss.

Rich wants to talk. He comes into the room where she's packing and leans against the door frame. For a while he says nothing; his eyes follow her from the closet to the cardboard boxes. Hers are labeled with only her initial, his with his full name and a list of the contents.

"How will you ever find anything?" he asks. "Do you want me to help you?"

"No thanks," she says. "Unpacking will be a surprise."

He fakes a shiver, shakes his chin back and forth. "How did we ever think this would work?"

She looks at him. "I'm not sure I ever did, to tell you the truth."

Outside the bedroom windows, two moving trucks are vying for space in the driveway. Their drivers are arguing loudly, in Spanish and hand gestures. With the curtains down the room is bright and bare; streaks show up in the paint, and a trail of smoke from a forgotten candle climbs the wall where her nightstand had been. The floor is dusty, strewn with duct tape; pieces of packing material litter the floor like unraveled cigar tobacco. In the window, the new pane of glass is oddly bright, unmarred by paint spatters, by fingerprints, by age. By comparison, the other panes seem dirty and smudged; the new owners will surely replace them.

"You were pretty easy at the closing," he says. He is rearranging the shoes she has tossed haphazardly into a tall box. He is balling up newspaper and stuffing the toes.

"At this point, you'd want to fight over how much oil is in the tank?"

He shrugs. "I mentioned the ducks to the wife."

"Rich," she says. "What is with you?"

"I feel worse than I thought I would is all. How about you?"

"I feel great. Relieved. Freed. I feel slightly less than a half a million bucks."

"Half that," he says.

"Right. Remind me to never again get married in a community property state."

He gives up. "I'm going to get going then. Before these guys kill each other out there."

He's not a man for backward glances, but she watches him just in case. He moves for the last time through the low doorways, steps outside, and kicks at a piece of flagstone that's come loose in the walkway. He has a word with the drivers; they laugh. He climbs into the open back of the moving truck and tugs at a few things to see if they're secure. Lila alternates the way she looks at him — first through the new glass, then through the old. Leaning on the sill, she sways slightly back and forth; her eyes adjust to each view, giving her a few instants of blurry vision, of dancing stars and motes of dust. He jumps down from the truck and braces his shoulders; she sees him climb into the cab.

She closes the last of the boxes up; the tape draws across the edges with a satisfying, final sound. Then she goes looking for the cat, who went underground when the commotion started. She finds him behind the washer, his sizable orange rump squeezed between hoses and cords. When she pulls him out, he looks at her with surprise; he'd never adjusted to her mother's death. He is still disappointed to find that Lila is the one holding him.

On a whim, she opens the French doors in the kitchen. The sun is glinting off the water; the ducks are preening themselves on the grass. The cat, having spent hours crying at the door, is too shocked, too torpid, to move quickly. He places one paw in the outside world and then retracts it. He does this several times. The ducks grow alarmed and begin to waddle quickly toward the water. Lila, finally, leans down and gives the cat a shove. After a moment he shakes himself off and begins to move across the lawn, lifting each paw with exaggerated care and then replacing it on grass — unfamiliar, damp, ticklish.

Lila locks the door; she leaves the square key in the lock. Several last wanders through the house are all that's left. Passing the living room windows, she sees the ducks lift off from the water. They are squawking angrily. They bank left to clear the house and are gone, leaving a faint fading cry.

Her mother's things fill the boxes that line the perimeters of the rooms; she's had no time, no room to collect her own. Her mother's furniture, her pictures, her treasures, Lila cannot seem to shed these things, this unwelcome inheritance. They are like her big knuckles, her bony wrists, her long fingers. More things her mother left her — a long list already, and growing.

In the bedroom, she balls her hand into a fist and raps her knuckles lightly on one of the old panes. The glazier, when he'd finally come, had pointed out the deteriorating seal; he'd warned that the other panes were a touch or two from falling out themselves. She counts fifteen panes right to left, excluding the new one. She starts at the top corner. She wants to hear shattering, to feel something slice her skin. She wants to notice the moment that contains the passage, the one that takes her from one place to the next.

Antique
Map
Collecting

Louisa faces a problem. Lying on the other side of the sloping glass window at the market is a trivial, everyday decision — salmon or filet of beef. The salmon — obscenely pink, striated, designed to flake at the touch of a fork tine — glistens on a bed of ice. Next to it the beef is humped and marbled, colored the deep red of organ meats.

Across from Louisa, the counterman is waiting, rubbing his hands on a stained butcher's apron. He is a fox-faced little man with disproportionately large hands. The counter reaches his neck so he is a little disembodied — his head directly across from hers, his hands and torso visible only through the glass — behind the offerings of meat and fish and poultry. Poultry, she thinks suddenly. I hadn't thought of it. A nice roasted bird, browned and crisp — who could object?

"So Louisa," the counterman says to her, "are you having guests?" His name is Don; she remembers that he has three children, a wife with back trouble. A collection had been taken up at the church to assist in some sort of expensive physical therapy. See there, she thinks. I'm not going round the bend just yet. I'm quite sharp.

To Don she says, "Yes. I haven't any idea what they like."

"Fish is nice," he says, "but salmon is a particular taste — not everyone's. You can't go wrong with a bird."

"Exactly what I was thinking," Louisa says and concludes the transaction. Behind her, the line is building. Someone bumps her arm with a basket; this shop provides heavy, quaint wicker baskets for gathering purchases. They are awkward and fill quickly; often you see people scuttling, bent over, down the aisles, chasing spilled tomatoes and oranges, like some queer bowling game. The store is, in this and other ways, charming but impractical. These days it is filled with young blonde housewives recently relocated from the city, dragging toddlers and ponytails behind them, dressed for tennis or lunch.

"How's it going with the house?" asks Don. He has come around the counter with the chicken, meaning to place it in the basket, but then he changes his mind and carries it up to the counter for her.

"Fine," she says. "The weather's been confusing, but I think it will come out all right. It's the bulbs I'm most worried about."

"Oh yes," he says, "your garden." He pats her arm and wishes her, of all things, good luck.

"You too," she says, thinking mainly of his wife. She wishes she'd remembered to say something sympathetic.

Louisa signs for her things — she is one of few people here who still do; the bill will arrive at the end of the month — and puts them neatly in the backseat of her car. She drives slowly, down familiar roads, taking all the trickier shortcuts.

On their street, she slows to watch the last of an old farmhouse come down. She holds a fist to her mouth — half the house is tinder now. Only the back wall remains, and she can see the guts of the old colonial, a fireplace against the rear wall. It's like looking inside a dollhouse, this view she has, the wainscoting running the length of the remaining wall, ending abruptly, jaggedly. Nearby, the house's remains are piled like matchsticks, like a child's game of building and destruction gone haywire, blown life-sized. This street was once lined with gracious old farmhouses, but now McMansions are sprouting in their place. These monstrosities— enormous, ridiculous—are being erected by the young blond families moving out from the city. What sort of people could do this? she wonders. People who need in-home theatres and basketball courts, gourmet kitchens big as bowling alleys. For a moment she stares, despising the people at both ends of these transactions, until a car honks behind her and she drives on.

Parked in the driveway, recently regraveled — the tires make a noise like breakfast cereal—she sits for a few moments. She passes a hand over her eyes. The garden is lovely at this time of day and year, with spring newly arrived and the pleated cups of the daffodils upturned and other hopeful things poking up out of the earth; inside the house, other problems await. Soldier on, she instructs herself. She unloads the groceries from the car and takes them inside.

It is four-thirty in the afternoon. She expects her husband at precisely five-fifteen. There will be no guests for dinner; they have not entertained for some time. Her husband is named Edward, and he works part-time at a real estate office. Sadly, this is all about him that Louisa can accurately remember. Recently, Louisa has begun to experience what she calls *slippage*. Facts — greasy as pigs at a fair, like apples bobbing and twisting in a barrel — are eluding her. Not trivial facts, like phone numbers or addresses or the dates of major battles and discoveries of continents, but a particular, isolated sort of fact. Edward-facts. Louisa has been married to Edward for forty-two years, and over the past month she has forgotten, or disremembered, each one of his likes and dislikes. All these escape her now: his inclinations and fondnesses, his antipathies, proclivities, his political positions and social leanings. These details, the large and insignificant alike, have been so thoroughly swept from her mind that they might never have existed there at all. Except for her vague knowledge of having once known these things, like a forgotten language which tickles at the back of your mind from time to time, coughing up a sudden useless, unasked-for detail — like the German word for train station (Bahnhof) or the word for a group of larks (exaltation) — Louisa might be married to a stranger. Once, she is sure, Edward's desires were as familiar as her own; her hands turned automatically in the motions that smoothed the bedclothes in the way he preferred, that folded underwear in the fashion he liked. Afternoons, standing over the laundry basket, she clutches socks and thinks: Rolled? Tops turned down together? Whatever could it be?

Because the one thing Louisa does remember about Edward is that he is fussy. He likes things just so. But, she wonders daily, *how* so is just so?

She is even surprised by the contours of his face, each evening. His figure emerging from the car in the driveway is a surprise; was he really that tall this morning when he left? My, hasn't he gone gray. Yesterday she had thought with surprise, My mother had insisted he'd be bald, but he isn't, not a bit.

This evening, as usual, Edward arrives at the kitchen door. She hears the bristling noise of his shoes scraping the mat and the quiet sound of give as the door opens; it reminds her that the catch needs fixing. Once inside, Edward will lift his nose immediately; three audible sniffs and then a comment will be forthcoming — a pronouncement: approval or disappointment and even, once or twice, sheer incredulity. This is the part of Louisa's day that has her on pins and needles.

"Chicken?" is what he says, in a thoughtful voice.

"Yes," says Louisa, drying her very dry hands on her skirt.

"Wonderful," he exclaims and immediately leaves the room — to change his clothes, to read the paper, to mix his own icy, amber drink from the tea cart, which has not carried a tea service for many years. She and Edward used to joke that her mother — an abstemious woman — must have been turning in the ground to see them lining up their decanters and the tantalus they had received as a wedding gift on the glass surface of this demure piece of furniture.

She hears Edward's voice from the other room — vexed.

"Yes?" she says and pokes her head around the corner. She has not even had one single moment to enjoy her success, to sigh against the counter with relief, to write *chicken* down on a scrap of paper and stuff it in a drawer, only to find it later and wonder, what's this? And then, is it chicken good or chicken bad?

"Why's this locked?" Edward is rattling at the small secure gates of the tantalus. The liquor bottles are held fast behind them, awaiting the click of a small ornate key.

"I can't imagine," Louisa says. She genuinely cannot. They have not employed servants for years. Edward's pension had been severely cut as a result of bad management by his previous employer, a company that publishes, among other things, those undersized magazines found in doctors' waiting rooms.

"Well, where's the key then?" Edward looks annoyed. He bends down to peer at the bottom rack of the tea cart. Louisa, following his eyes, sees that the caning needs attention; there are a number of fraying bits. He straightens up and looks at her again, spreads his hands open and lifts them ever so slightly. Everyone, even Louisa, knows what this gesture means.

"I haven't touched the thing," she says, but walks over and lets her eyes travel across the top rack. The key — a small iron one with a curlicued head and a small piece of brown silk ribbon attached — is nowhere in sight. She tugs at the little wooden gates, like miniature castle doors. They hold.

"Well," she says.

"Well, what?"

It is hard to say with whom Louisa is most irritated at the moment: herself, for forgetting everything important, or Edward, for somehow being the cause of it; which she suspects, though there is no evidence to support it.

In any case, she puts her hands on the two little gates and gives them a fierce yank. No one is more surprised than she when the wood and metal utter a little shriek; a ripping noise and the gates fall open, one completely off its hinge — the interior mechanism of the lock visible through splintered wood.

"Voilà," she says to him, in a voice that trembles only slightly. She reaches inside and withdraws the three heavy crystal decanters, sets them one by one on the cart with a small clunking sound.

"My God." he says. "Good grief. What are you thinking? Louisa, have you lost your mind? That was a gift from my grandmother."

"No," she says. "It was a gift from mine."

"It never was," says Edward, stubbornly. "Never. My grandmother Helen gave this to us. I remember it as a boy, sitting on the china buffet."

"You were, or it was?" says Louisa. She is breathing heavily. She moves the decanters so that they sit in a neat, exact line, with their diamond-cut edges paralleling each other.

Then, for no reason other than perversity, she says, "Your grandmother Helen was a witch, truth be told. I always despised her. She never had a nice word to say about anything or anyone."

"No. She just never had a nice word to say about you." Edward is holding the ice tongs and dropping cubes — one, two, three — into a heavy tumbler.

Louisa reaches her hand out, chooses a decanter, and pulls the stopper. She pours — carelessly — two fingers into his glass. He stares at her.

He says, "What are you doing? That's bourbon."

Louisa asks her friends: Tell me, do you ever forget things? Every day, they say. My handbag, where my car is, my head if it wasn't screwed on. No, really. Important things. I think I may be going mad. In this manner, she solicits a number of strange, off-topic admissions from her friends.

Virginia recounts a dream she had some while ago about a garden party. Gwen tells them of a holiday she once took to the Italian coast, an incident in an airport. Neither of these stories addresses Louisa's question; their conversations have been veering off like this lately.

That's not at all what I mean, Louisa told them, puzzled. They were having soup at the time, the three of them. Virginia and Gwen and Louisa. Their friendship had taken them places, over the years. They had been girlhood friends and then girlhood enemies and, finally, mothers and wives, living in sympathetic proximity.

Louisa leans forward; her hair is a helmet of tight, sprayed curls. When her head moves her hair does not. "It's Edward," she says. "Just him. Everything else I remember entirely."

"Bully for you," says Virginia, whose husband shoved her around until he overworked himself doing it and had a heart attack.

Gwen says, "Count your blessings." She lifts slender eyebrows. Gwen is on her third husband; old whatshisbucket, Virginia and Louisa call him.

Louisa rests her elbows on the table and sighs. "Walnuts," she says. "How did they feel about them?" Last week she had baked a banana bread; the look on Edward's face when he had speared one with his fork is still with her.

Imagine, says Louisa, what that's like. The not knowing. The two women wag their heads at her. Funny how Louisa feels so much younger, so much more likely to meet a cowboy, or a motorcycle rider, and wave off into the sunset. She'd be one of those ancient women in leather pants, a chest like crepe paper, with streaked, straggling hair. She imagines this for a moment: her spotted hands clutching the waist of some Hell's Angel, the long-forgotten taste of cold beer, this faceless man's wiry ponytail catching in her lipstick. Absurd.

Gwen says, "Well, it's time I told you. You must have noticed. I had a facelift in the winter, when I said I was visiting my sister."

"Of course," say Louisa and Virginia together, "that explains it."

Later that night on the telephone, they will say to each other, Too little, too late. And why does she always bring up that damned trip to Europe, like she's the only one who's ever left the state?

───────

In the mornings, when Edward's left the house, Louisa prowls it restlessly. She walks the gardens, bending to examine the progress of spring. At her potting table, she is nursing along tomato plants in tiny earthen cups; each has one tiny green shoot with two leaves. As the days wane, these two leaves, responding to some instinct, some nuance of light, fold up their tiny leaves like praying hands. All is going as planned, according to schedule. The peonies, with their red stalks and closed, shaggy buds, are getting taller by the day. The lilies are green stars shooting up behind the boxwoods, in the shade they prefer. There is dill in the herb garden, reddening leaves on the roses, and vinca is spreading under the apple trees.

The calendar warns her that Edward's birthday is approaching. It's news she takes quite seriously, with a good deal of apprehension. She phones her daughter one morning. Jane lives on the West Coast and has a high-powered job having to do with other people's money. Louisa has never really understood it, how this child — this clumsy, careless, helpless baby — has managed to become a woman with a closet full of severe business suits and a kitchen made entirely of stainless steel.

Louisa, as usual, speaks for a few minutes to Jane's secretary — another thing she can't quite get over, women with secretaries — and gives a general, largely false accounting of her health and well-being. In the polite world of business in which Jane lives, on the highest floor of some mirrored skyscraper, Jane is careful to treat her secretary with reserved friendliness. At Christmas they exchange scarves and expensive, benign bottles of lotions and bath salts. Jane is always careful to spend enough but not too much, reflecting her salary and position without seeming overdone or signaling any desire for a more equal relationship. Louisa knows this only because Jane has told her, has agonized with her over the telephone for weeks leading up to Christmas and birthdays, wanting to know: What might this gift mean? Or that one? Too personal or impersonal; too expensive or cheap? It's the memory of these conversations that has prompted Louisa to call Jane about Edward's birthday. She has considered the conversation carefully, and when Jane picks up the telephone — in a rush, as usual — Louisa delivers her opening line.

"Tell me, dear, do you remember what I got Edward for his birthday last year?"

"What?" Jane says, and then, "Oh. Sure."

It isn't what Louisa had hoped for. "Do you think he liked it?" she tries.

"Daddy? Who knows. He's so difficult."

This is hopeful and, Louisa says, "Do you think so?"

"Is there anyone who doesn't think so?" says Jane. Louisa can hear her tapping away on a computer keyboard.

"Well," says Louisa, "What were you thinking of getting him this year?"

"Me?" says Jane. "Nothing. Have you forgotten that he and I are at war?"

She has, of course. "Still?" she asks. "Isn't it time to put that behind you?"

There is a long silence. "Mother," says Jane, "Are you feeling all right?"

"Perfectly fine," she replies. "Tickety-boo. But I should let you go, I know you're busy, busy."

"Don't be patronizing," says Jane, and then says, more gently, "Do take care of yourself, will you? I'll call soon."

Louisa replaces the receiver and sighs. Lately, all her conversations have this cryptic, gently probing quality. It reminds her of years ago, when they gave and attended parties, and Gwen, having always had too much to drink, would next morning tiptoe around the evening's events, trying to gauge just how awful she'd been. Her voice on the telephone would be falsely bright, circling, looking for details and trespasses, finding out if apologies were called for.

Louisa, still in her dressing gown, pads upstairs and conducts a thorough search of Edward's closet. The contents seem mysterious, belonging as they do to this near stranger. There is a very large collection of dated ties; Edward doesn't wear them anymore, as the real estate business is rather casual. His shoes are treed and polished; the mahogany drawers hold his very white, carefully folded underthings. Beneath them, she finds various bits and pieces — a receipt or two, an old money clip, some foreign coins so old as to no longer be in currency.

Downstairs again, she stands in the doorway of his study and surveys it. Three walls are book-lined; the two antique French smoking chairs are tilted toward each other in a conversational arrangement, though as far as she knows, no one but Edward has ever sat in either of them. She scans the bottom shelves of the bookcases, the taller shelves that hold coffee table–sized books, the sort with pictures and illustrations that might indicate a person's hobby or avocation. She notices a theme and steps into the room to examine a collection of books that have to do with maps and cartography. *Antique Map Collecting*, one is called, and others have similar titles. She flips one open and rifles the pages. The book opens to pale charted pages, scalloped drawings of round maps laid flat, veined with pastel tracings no wider than a fingernail's edge. Some show shipping routes of long ago, indicated in black; others name places no longer in the world's vernacular. She replaces the book and finds, framed on the wall, a particularly lovely old map, under a small lamp made for spotlighting art. She lifts it away from the wall and turns it over in her hands. A small plaque — brass — reads: *To Edward from Lou. I'm so glad to be traveling this life with you.*

Louisa is surprised at herself. She doesn't remember being this sappy, or romantic. She can no longer distinguish any difference between the two. The date is many years earlier; they would have been married only a few years. How did she afford such a thing? More important, is Edward still interested in maps?

She returns the picture to the wall with great care and closes the door of his study behind her. There was a time, she recalls, when he locked the door of this room. In the evenings he would close himself inside and work at condensing volumes of literature, his profession at the time. They argued over it. It seemed obscene to Louisa — this compressing and scrunching of great books into digestible morsels for lazy readers. How can they say they've read such and such a book, she'd say, outraged, when they've just swallowed your freeze-dried version? She was equally indignant, years later, when people began listening to books while driving in their cars. But Edward took this work quite seriously, vested, he felt, with the power to make literature accessible to the general public. It was a subject about which he could be quite contentious — either because he saw nothing wrong with it or because it was what he was paid to do. Louisa was never certain. Gwen, she remembers, had liked to engage him in debates about the subject; she would bait him along, wide-eyed and interested, before pouncing and exposing him. Once she had called him a hack, and he hadn't spoken to her for months.

This would have been at the end of their affair, when they were looking for reasons and opportunities to despise each other. It's a time Louisa remembers well. It was Edward's sullenness that had tipped her off, his going out of his way to find fault with Gwen. It had seemed to Louisa an unnatural animosity — one that signaled more emotion than was seemly toward a friend of one's wife, a mere social acquaintance. Of course, she had caught them together that once, at the tired, tail end of some party, roughing each other up in the kitchen. When she had stepped around the doorway, they had foolishly fallen against each other, not away, and then shoved at each other in a ridiculous, childish way, catching at sleeves and banging hips against the sink. Louisa had laughed; it was that silly. Anyway, there had been a lot of that going on at the time; people looked the other way. An artist, or a satirist, might have depicted it in this way: a dozen or so well-heeled couples staring off in different directions, fixing their eyes on the drapes, or the olive plate, or pointing out the crown moldings, whilst leering figures with enlarged private parts cavorted at their feet, under their upturned noses. In any case, that was how Louisa thought of it. The day after that party, when Gwen's voice — timid and defensive — came across the phone line, Louisa had said nothing about it. And confronting Edward would not have occurred to her.

Louisa's revenge affair had not really worked out any better. It had been a boring, listless episode with Jane's pediatrician, often consummated on the floor of his office, while bright yellow ducks and cottontailed bunnies looked down from the wallpaper and mobiles of airships swayed overhead. These interludes carry in Louisa's mind certain accompanying sensory experiences — the smell of baby and antiseptic, the sounds of whimpering and sniffling, or, on inoculation days, of ear-splitting wails as his nurse jabbed baby after baby in the room next door. The guilt she felt revolved mostly around Jane and a mounting feeling that the child — only a toddler at the time — might somehow, when she learned to talk, suddenly burst out with some revelation at the dinner table. Louisa had even kissed him in front of Jane, while the little girl sat quietly on the examining table, bending tongue depressors. In the end, it was too great a risk for too little reward, and when she had delivered the news to him — during a routine examination, of which Jane had more than her fair share — he had straightened up from peering into Jane's ear and said: "I agree completely. Thank you for being so grown-up about it." And Louisa was left with the feeling that she had been the one jilted rather than the other way around. Then, as they looked at each other, taking the sort of stock that parting lovers will — never see that part of him or her again, never smell their hair or neck, touch that freckle — Jane had suddenly piped up in an angry voice and said, "Cold!" They stared at her. He had forgotten to take the scope from her ear and Jane was sick of the chilly metal point of it. They had laughed then, and Louisa had said, "Well, there you go. Her first word, a complaint!"

He said, "Like mother, like daughter." And then she had had to wonder about that too.

Louisa is pleased. Outside the kitchen window, the goldfinches have appeared. There is the constant, industrious noise they make, building nests in the rose trellises, in the straw hat she hung years ago for just such a purpose. Just beyond the feeders the lilacs are creeping with color. Soon they will spill blossoms all over the house; she will happily sweep them up from the kitchen counters, the hall table, the bathrooms, where she will have set individual spikes into Limoges cups.

She is humming a little, moving around the kitchen. Since chicken had been a hit, and she has miraculously remembered it, she prepares it again. She digs up her mother's carrot cake recipe and spends the afternoon whipping cream cheese with sugar. She also remembers to leave the walnuts out. She congratulates herself. Maybe, she thinks, this will turn out to be a passing malady — like a pain you ride out, hoping not to have to go to the doctor and be diagnosed with something terminal.

When Edward comes home at his usual time, he says very quickly, even before the door has closed behind him, "What's that I smell?"

"Roast chicken," says Louisa. She is carefully spreading frosting on the cake, which has turned out quite beautifully.

"Not again," he says. "You know I can't eat the same thing twice in one week."

No, she thinks, I didn't.

"People do," she tells him.

"Not this one," he says. "Can't you do something else?"

"There's carrot cake."

She's sick of it. Now that Edward's wishes are inscrutable, no longer a part of her hands' or mind's recollections, she sees that he's a pill. She says, "Tell me, Edward, have you always been like this?"

"Like what?" He is standing across the wooden island in the kitchen, taking a glass down from the cabinet.

"Difficult. As Jane would put it."

"Jane!" he says. "Her. Have you two spoken?"

"Recently," she says. "And you should resolve whatever this is between you."

He stares at her. "I consider it resolved. Don't you?"

"I don't believe so," she says firmly, but still, she leaves the room quickly and thinks up something to do in the laundry room.

When she comes back, she finds Edward sitting on the old church pew in the mudroom, pulling up his rubber boots. His drink sits next to him, leaking a wet circle onto the mail. The pile is quite high and she needs to go through it; every day she tosses it here on her way into the house and promptly forgets about it. She sees envelopes with cellophane windows, flyers from the supermarket, official-looking notices gathering rings from their nightly duty as coasters.

"Lou," he says. "There you are. I'm going to have a look at the back garden. That should give you time to think something else up for dinner."

She says to him, "Edward, have you ever thought that you are just the tiniest bit relentless?"

"Jane?" is what he says, not looking up, concentrating on pulling up the second boot. He grunts deep in his throat, slaps the sides of the boot.

"No," she tells him. "Louisa."

He stands and opens the mudroom door that leads into the back garden. She watches him through the window, walking out past the low picket gate, down the long length of grass, past the peony bank and the birch trees, beyond the wooden swing that hangs from the gnarled limb of their oldest apple tree, the pink one, until he fades into the shadows of the cypress. Just a little farther, she knows, is the chain gate that leads to the marshy bit of their land, another acre or more, a place where she had once thought to put in a tennis court, but Edward decided instead to shore up with rocks and drainage, to make it suitable for something else. This thought, suddenly, gives Louisa a disturbing headache: a prickling behind her eyebrows that feels quite ominous, like a signal or warning of something terrible, a sort of pain semaphore or mayday. Fortunately, she has no idea what it might be and, instead, rubs at the places with her fingertips and returns to the kitchen, thinking of a casserole she might have frozen, once.

There, she runs her fingers along the marbled sink, a mosaic she had ordered from Italy, long ago. Its colors — brilliant cobalt and yellow and green — cheer her daily. She walks the rooms again: the fireplace in the kitchen, dating from revolutionary days, its cooking paraphernalia — an iron pot hanging on a swinging arm — still intact. A fireplace she can stand up inside. The bookcase that disguises a secret passage—a mere turn of tightly wound steps — to the living room. Now she steps out and closes the door behind her. Another fireplace, encased in an enormous wooden mantle. The soft light of the lamps, the worn oriental rugs, the fraying furniture. The windows! She'd forgotten for a moment. Deep windows, leaded casements, winding out on creaky, cranky handles. Opening out to riotous gardens, growing willy-nilly in a way that Edward hates. Yes! she remembers that — he hates the wild profusion of flowers, the lack of neatness and order, the disheveled flowers and greenery.

Peering out in the fading light, she sees something wrong. Beyond the hedges and the bosky woods, something is glinting, leaning, at the end of the willows, half-hidden by fountains of forsythia.

Louisa puts on her gardening gloves and walks the length of the driveway. She bends and shoves the thing upright. It turns out to be a metal sign, listing now. It says: *Sold.* She yanks it out of the ground and tosses it, rusted metal legs and all, onto the road. In faded letters, at the lower part of the sign, she reads this: *Edward Thatcher, Licensed Agent.*

And now, something comes to her. First, it is the look on the face of the butcher, tallying up her purchases, swinging endless chickens over the counter, walking her to the front and whispering something to the clerk. Is she imagining that glances follow her out of the market? When did they last pay that bill? It is Edward, disappearing in the mornings, mixing drinks with water to make them stretch, raising his eyebrows if he comes home to a good cut of meat, or a piece of fish. Chicken! she thinks suddenly — he's been making a joke.

It is Jane, at Easter, looking around the house and saying, "Take the money, Dad, won't you? Don't be so goddam stubborn."

Edward had said no. He said it just once, but it was enough. That look crossed his face — pride, defeat, mulishness.

Louisa kneels in the garden. She puts her hands in the dirt and lifts it to her face. She is thinking of places where the earth is not loamy and soft; she is thinking of sand and of plants so self-sufficient that her ministrations won't be needed, ugly vegetation that grows spitefully and is likely to hurt you. She thinks of water so blue it looks hard as stone, of relentless sunlight and communal meals and Friday-evening dances in a cafeteria that smells of overcooked vegetables. Of Edward's desire for a simpler life, one that does not require bending and squatting in gardens, clearing muck from gutters, caring for trees. In the dusky light she examines her hands — splotched now from years of gardening, from nursing along those dastardly peonies, from making surgical cuts on the rose bushes, leaving three leaves, always, never just two.

She thinks of Jane — her unaccountably capable daughter — born in this very house. She remembers the tantalus suddenly, and where she had hidden the key. At the bottom of a cup that holds one infant tomato plant; the bit of brown ribbon probably still pokes from the drainage. Of course, it was Helen's gift. It always was. But more than that, it was something Edward loved, admired, showed off. She feels a climbing, wretched shame.

She is there when Edward finds her. When he sinks creakily down and says, "What would you like me to do? Take money from our daughter?"

She realizes then that there have been a thousand recent conversations that began this way, and she glances at him, looking for clues. She thinks it has been mostly an accident, their years of marriage, their living together all this time. She'd never thought it might turn out like this; she'd been waiting for life to offer up something else, to whisk her off in some adventure or romance, to present circumstances beyond her control. That life has snubbed her in this respect — and it is nearly impossible, at this moment, to think otherwise — is a cruel surprise.

Kneeling there, the two of them, in gardening clothes — Louisa's straw hat pushed back so the cord strafes her throat — he reaches for her hand. They sit in silence for an interminable time.

Louisa is thinking of Edward a month earlier, jolly and businesslike, stepping from his car, handing out a blonde woman in a ponytail, in khaki pants and a headscarf. The woman's husband had followed in another car; he stepped out — instantly appraising — then wrenched a toddler from the backseat. Their progress through the house was swift, judging. The woman admired the gardens, the years of backbreaking work. Louisa had thought, following at a safe distance, listening, As though I'd done it for her. The husband twittered about the lack of modern things, the furnace, the outdated appliances, the hand-cranked windows, the soft floors, planks too wide for a single step.

Edward had said, "Don't you agree? The land is spectacular. Not to be replicated. Not to be found."

The husband nodded; the wife tore the baby away from the herb garden, where he was ripping silvery sage from the ground, rubbing the velvety leaves on his cheek.

Edward said, "It's zoned, of course. It can come down entirely if that's what you want. You could always build on, though."

They stood at the car — the husband, the wife, the toddler. Louisa stood a short distance away, bending over cornflowers, half-listening.

The husband — pink, blond, overfed — said, "Well, yes. We'll take it down. These old houses are so cramped. Have you seen what they're doing these days? The builders? It will be spectacular. Hope you don't feel sentimental."

"No," Edward had said, "Not at all. Raze away. We're going south. Happy to be done with it, frankly."

They drove away in their glinting silver car. Louisa watched the woman drinking water from a bottle, tossing her blonde head in some discussion.

Now, feeling Edward's hand in hers — cracked, dry, all knuckles — Louisa remembers the armloads of soft flowers she has nursed and carried for years upon years, the praying leaves of seedlings, the china-blue vases on the wraparound porch, holding masses and masses of roses, of peonies, of hydrangea, all summer long.

Louisa looks at Edward. She believes he is dreaming of golf courses and air-conditioned shopping malls, of friends he will make to play bridge with, of all-you-can-eat restaurants, where he can — really can — choose something different every night of the week. But really, she has no idea. And anyway, she thinks — a thought that strikes with a sudden, surprising force — it doesn't even matter anymore, not at all.

The Iowa Short Fiction Award and John Simmons Short Fiction Award Winners

1991
The Ant Generator,
Elizabeth Harris

Traps, Sondra Spatt Olsen

1990
A Hole in the Language,
Marly Swick

1989
Lent: The Slow Fast,
Starkey Flythe, Jr.

Line of Fall, Miles Wilson

1988
The Long White,
Sharon Dilworth

The Venus Tree,
Michael Pritchett

1987
Fruit of the Month,
Abby Frucht

Star Game, Lucia Nevai

1986
Eminent Domain,
Dan O'Brien

Resurrectionists,
Russell Working

1985
Dancing in the Movies,
Robert Boswell

1984
Old Wives' Tales,
Susan M. Dodd

1983
Heart Failure, Ivy Goodman

1982
Shiny Objects, Dianne Benedict

1981
The Phototropic Woman,
Annabel Thomas

1980
Impossible Appetites,
James Fetler

1979
Fly Away Home, Mary Hedin

1978
A Nest of Hooks, Lon Otto

1977
The Women in the Mirror,
Pat Carr

1976
The Black Velvet Girl,
C. E. Poverman

1975
*Harry Belten and the
Mendelssohn Violin Concerto,*
Barry Targan

1974
*After the First Death There Is No
Other,* Natalie L. M. Petesch

1973
The Itinerary of Beggars,
H. E. Francis

1972
The Burning and Other Stories,
Jack Cady

1971
*Old Morals, Small Continents,
Darker Times,*
Philip F. O'Connor

1970
The Beach Umbrella,
Cyrus Colter

Alan Haywood

Beth Helms was born in
California and grew up in
the Middle East and Europe.
She is a graduate of Vermont
College's MFA Writing
Program and currently
lives in Pound Ridge,
New York.